by
Eve Langlais

Copyright © June 2011, Eve Langlais
Cover Art by Amanda Kelsey © June 2011
Edited by Victoria Miller
Produced in Canada

Published by Eve Langlais
Suite 126 — 2377 Hwy #2 Unit 120
Bowmanville ON, L1C 5E2
www.EveLanglais.com

ISBN13 : 978 146 369 8409
ISBN 10: 146 3698 402

Chapter One

He's a freakn' beast.

Naomi watched in rapt fascination as player number forty-four scored yet another goal. Like an implacable freight train, he plowed through the opposition's defense as if they didn't exist, using his size, and surprising speed, to bowl them over. At the end of his shift, he went to sit his turn on the bench, but her fascination in the game didn't waver. Her attention ended up snagged by player sixty-nine. Smaller in stature than the behemoth, he absorbed her just as completely with his feline grace as he twisted and moved around the floor. He almost danced as he ran, his stick held high and usually cradling the ball.

What is it about the two of them that fascinates me? I don't even like lacrosse. And she hated jocks.

Naomi still couldn't believe she'd allowed her friend, Francine, to talk her into coming to watch a lacrosse game. She usually left contact sports and their watching of to her father and brothers, preferring games of intellectual skill and preciseness, like curling or golf. However, a free ticket, and nothing better to do on a Saturday night, along with a promise by Francine to go dancing afterward, swayed her. Thus, she found herself a spectator, seated about twelve rows up, just above the protective glass. With her enhanced sense of smell, she could catch occasional whiffs of the sweat glistening on the players' skin, the musky aroma not at all repulsive like she expected. She reluctantly admitted—if only to herself— the impressive speed and strength displayed by the lacrosse players—two in particular—made her girly parts tingle. Even more surprising, something about these males made her inner wolf yip in excitement.

Ignoring her bitch's griping, she returned her focus to the game, but her brow crinkled as she found herself unable to divert her attention from either the behemoth or the lithe runner. Her wolf wouldn't let her, even when they both sat on the bench. *This is not a good sign.* Naomi fidgeted, trying not to stare at the two players, but unbidden, her gaze kept straying back.

Francine must have caught on to something because she whispered. "What's wrong? You look like you just swallowed a lemon? And did I just hear you growl?"

A frown crossed Naomi's face. "Yeah, I growled. It's not my fault though. Something's got my wolf in a tizzy." Naomi shrugged, pushing aside her unease as her eyes swiveled to track the behemoth who had exited the bench and now ran across the floor again. Warmth suffused her at the raw power he exuded as he body checked an opposing player—*I wonder if he's as active in bed?* Naomi's scowl widened at the train of her thoughts. "Maybe it's all the violence or something making my bitch agitated."

A snort escaped Francine. "You're kidding, right? On a good day, your family makes these guys look like pussy cats."

Naomi bit her lip as she thought of the males of her clan whose idea of a discussion usually resulted in bloodshed, sore knuckles and black eyes. "Okay, you might have a point. But still, there's something in the air or crowd that's agitating my wolf."

Francine clutched Naomi's arm in a tight vise and turned a face lit with excitement toward her. "Hey, maybe your wolf is sensing your mate in the arena."

Mate? Naomi's surge of warm pleasure at number sixty-nine's pirouette and dash shriveled as she gazed

4

around at all the big and brash men in the crowd. Shifters, of course. Mere humans could try all they wanted to attend one of their sold out lacrosse exhibitions, only those who could claim an animal in their ancestry could attend. The privately owned gymnasium they used for their clan sports was owned and operated by those of her kind. Sports provided a civilized way for them to express their more volatile side. And a profitable one as she well knew since she did their accounting.

Francine's assertion that her mate could, in fact, be one of these violence-loving, meatheads left her cold. She shivered, not in fear but repugnance. "No thank you. The idea of getting hitched to a Neanderthal makes me want to puke."

Her best friend rolled her eyes. "Oh, come on. You can't tell me you're still thinking of going through with your plan."

Naomi lifted her shoulders again instead of answering. The plan her friend spoke of involved marrying a nice—very normal—human male and living a mundane and drama—AKA brawl—free life. Not that she'd ever had any violence directed at her—although she'd caused some on occasion when she lost her temper, usually on one of her burly brothers. Her father and siblings would never let anyone, themselves included, harm a hair on her head, but amongst each other, fists spoke more often than words. As the only girl with five older, testosterone laden brothers, Naomi learned early how to hold her ground and retaliate when they pulled their pranks. Having grown up in chaos, where a wrestling match could break out at any moment, she decided years ago that at least in her case, marrying a shifter prone to chaotic episodes because of their animal nature wasn't her idea of a happily ever after. While the bedlam didn't seem to bother her mother, or even her female shifter friends, Naomi longed for peace and quiet—and the ability to own crystal.

In her childhood home, none of the dishes matched and furniture was butt ugly given sturdy didn't equal pretty. In her parent's house, things needed to withstand just about any kind of natural—or familial—disaster. Currently living on her own, Naomi's place reflected the exact opposite, with elegant pieces in light colors. She especially cherished her fragile collection of glass butterflies, and gleefully enjoyed the fact none of them had required crazy glue after a particularly frenzied family event. She didn't miss having to referee her brothers by grabbing hold of their ears and tweaking them into submission. She hated all the male posturing and ball scratching assertion the males of the shifter clans required. *Gentle and normal, that's all I ask for.*

Given her desires, Francine's suggestion that her mate could possibly be in attendance at this bloodthirsty and brutal sporting event filled her with horror. Although, what if some quirk of fate brought the shifter in question—an intellectual type who preferred discourse to pugilism—to the lacrosse match by accident, much like herself? She snorted. *Fat chance.*

An "Ooh" from the crowd drew her from her thoughts and she looked up to see someone from the London team splayed out on the floor, flattened by number forty-four, the behemoth from their very own house team, the Ottawa city, Loup Garou's.

The Loup Garou's—which translated to werewolf, even if the team was comprised of a dozen species—hollered in triumph as their main man sprang over the prone body of the hapless opposing player. The titan sprinted for the opposite end, his broad body and shoulders acting the part of blocker and clearing a path. Number sixty-nine, with a Colgate grin that made her shiver, paralleled the behemoth, the ball cradled in his lacrosse cage as he dodged the pissed off Londoners, those still left standing after the beast's rush.

As a new team, the London Moon Shifters were still digging hard to acquire players tough enough to stand against the older teams. Actually, according to her brothers, because of the behemoth and his slimmer compatriot, all the teams currently scrambled to find players that could break the Loup Garou's winning streak. Transferred to the team from Saskatchewan in only the last month, the acquisitions of the two best players by her home city was quite the buzz around town. Her brothers crowed about it and wrestled each other in their excitement. Naomi personally thought the concept of paying guys to throw a ball around and hit each other with sticks was dumb. *So dumb, yet I can't stop watching,* she thought with disgust.

The play on the floor moved fast as the clock ticked down to victory. In a last ditch effort, two of the bigger London players ran in a bull rush at number sixty-nine, who grinned before he sprang into the air with feline agility and fired the ball at a speed humans would have choked at. The giant, still running swiftly, moved to intercept the ball currently tunneling through the air.

The crowd hushed as they watched athleticism at its finest, including Naomi, whose wolf forced her to stare with rapt attention. A man his size, more so than the rest of the population, should have remained subject to the laws of gravity and yet, despite his obvious height and weight, when the behemoth leapt—his ascent almost vertical—he soared like the lightest of feathers.

Leaning forward, with her breath held, she waited for nature's rules to drag the beast—dressed in a delectable man's body—back down, even as she knew second hand from her brothers —fanatic lacrosse fans— the man kept defying the odds. Up he soared, his netted stick rising high above his head, reaching to grab the ball whipping through the air. The crowd stopped breathing, their bodies taut with tension. For a moment, number forty-four's eyes, the surprising soft brown of a wren's feather, met hers—and locked.

The breath sucked from her lungs at the intense, yet puzzled, regard in his surprisingly beautiful orbs, framed by thick dark lashes. Heat coiled low in her tummy as his slow curling smile tugged at her own lips and shot a tingling, wet warmth to her cleft.

Suddenly, his eyes rounded in horror and his mouth opened on a yell a second before he smacked into the arena glass like a bug on a windshield. She didn't really get a chance to enjoy his cartoon splatting moment because she blacked out as their dual moment of inattention saw her smacked in the face by the game ball as it torpedoed into it.

Chapter Two

Ethan slumped on the bench in the change room, ignoring the ribald behavior around him after yet another foregone win. A hard slap on the rear of his head roused him and he whirled, his lip curled back as he growled menacingly.

"Don't you dare show me your teeth," Javier warned with a dark look. He ran his hand through hair, already tousled and sweaty from the match. "What the fuck happened out there? I passed you the perfect shot, and instead of grabbing it and scoring, you crashed into the goddamn arena glass. What are you, a rookie? Been watching too many Bugs Bunny cartoons?"

Heat burned Ethan's cheeks in remembrance of his mishap before dejection—along with a large dose of disbelief—quickly set back in. "I missed. It happens and besides, it's not like we needed the point to win."

"Of course we didn't," Javier replied with a scoffing snort. "But it's the point of it. What the hell distracted you so much? And, why do you look like your best friend died, which, I might add, is an impossibility given I'm standing right beside you." Javier grinned.

"I think I found my mate," Ethan muttered. A true beauty with light skin, a perfect oval face framed by long, brown hair and the most perfect set of rosebud lips.

Javier's face expressed shock, then glee. "Congrats, dude." Javier slapped him hard on the back, and while the blow might have killed a human or a smaller species, it didn't even budge Ethan. "I know you've been pining to settle down with someone of the fairer sex. You must be ecstatic."

"Not really." Although he should have been. Finding one's mate was a one in a zillion chance given how shifters were scattered across the globe. Most never even came close to finding the one fate deemed their perfect match.

His friend's jovial grin subsided. "What's wrong? Was she, like, butt ugly? Humongous? Old? Surely she can't be that bad?"

"No, she appears perfect. Or did." Ethan groaned as banged his head off the locker door. "I am so screwed."

A frown creased Javier's face. "I don't get it. I thought you wanted to find *the one*, you sick bastard. Settle down and pop out cubs." Ethan looked up in time to see Javier's mock shudder. "Me, I prefer to share my love among as many women as possible." Javier mimed slapping an ass then humping it with a leering grin.

Ethan didn't smile at Javier's attempt at humor even if it happened to be the truth. Javier certainly enjoyed variety where the other sex was concerned. Heck, on many an occasion he'd shared with Ethan. Tag team sessions where they both scored. Best friends who did just about everything together.

Blowing out a long sigh, Ethan answered him. "I do want to find my mate, actually, I'm pretty sure I already have, but I don't think I made a great impression. She's the one they took out on the stretcher after the ball I missed hit her in the face."

Javier winced. "Ouch. Sucks to be you, my friend. Don't worry, though. I'm sure she'll forgive you in, like, fifty years."

Ethan groaned and dropped his head back into his hands. *Now that I've found her, how do I discover who she is so I can beg her forgiveness?*

And even worse, how the hell do I act the part of suitor?

Raised in the Alaskan wilds by a father who wasn't all there after the death of Ethan's mother, his education in social niceties was sadly lacking. He tended to speak with his fists more often than not. Lucky for him, when it came to women, he didn't usually have to do a thing. Females tended to approach him for sex so they could brag afterward that they'd ridden the Kodiak and survived. Not that Ethan would ever hurt a female, even if his idea of flirty conversation usually consisted of "Suck me harder" and "Bend over." *If I add "darling" on the end, will she count it as sweet talk?*

Actually, he should probably preface anything he said with a humungous sorry. Make that a few thousand apologies given the hit she'd suffered proved spectacular enough to make the crowd "Ooh" in harmony.

Perhaps he panicked over nothing. After all, the woman his inner bear chuffed was his mate had attended a lacrosse game. Shouldn't that imply she knew the risks? That she didn't mind a bit of blood and violence? Besides, as a shifter, she'd heal quickly. He could only pray and hope his pragmatism ended up as reality.

As for the whole courting thing, if fate deemed the woman his perfect match, then surely his intended wouldn't let something like his lack of manners deter her from giving in to the inevitable. *Then again, I could always resort to my dad's tactics which involve throwing her over my shoulder and dragging her back to the woods for some loving, mountain man style.*

He was getting ahead of himself though, because for all he knew he worried over nothing. Chances were she couldn't wait to meet him as well. Most female shifters—or so he'd heard—lived for the day they encountered their mate. *And lucky her, she's found me.*

His inner pep talk didn't entirely banish his unease as he stripped out of the rest of his equipment. The after game ritual, though, calmed him and a plan formed in his mind.

"I need to find out who she is," he told Javier as he entered the shower room with the rest of the team. "If they had to take her out on a stretcher, then chances are someone knows her name."

"Good for you, my friend, for not giving up in the face of obvious adversity. And because I am such a good friend, I shall come with you when you visit her so I might laugh when the female retaliates against you for messing up her face."

Javier flew backward with the force of the punch Ethan laid on him. Rubbing his jaw, his friend glared up at him. "That wasn't very nice."

Ethan snarled. "Maybe if you hadn't thrown the ball so damned hard, I wouldn't be in this position in the first place. I'm glad you find my situation so goddamned funny."

Jumping to his feet, Javier raised his fists. "Alright, my friend. Let's go. You obviously need to work off some tension, might as well do it now. Think of your coming beating as a courting favor because I'm going to give you some black eyes to match those of your mate."

"I'd like to see you try." With a feral grin, Ethan lumbered at his friend, paws swinging as the other players in the shower room scattered.

Old habits died hard, and when it came to working out frustration, the easiest route still involved violence. Ethan refused to view it as stalling out of fear. Kodiak bears feared nothing, especially not one fated female. But just in case, perhaps once he de-stressed, he would pick up flowers, or buy a whole damned floral shop for her.

* * * * *

Naomi, ensconced on the sturdy family couch, held the ice pack to her throbbing face and listened with only half an ear as her family fought. Francine—the crowing and snickering bitch—had escaped and left her to the *tender* mercies of her family.

"I'll teach that fucking lacrosse player to not pay attention to the game and let our sister get hurt," Derrick ranted punching his fist into the palm of his other hand.

"I say we hunt bloody forty-four and sixty-nine down. Let's tie their asses up and whip some rubber balls at their face and see how they like it," yelled Stu. "Who's with me?" A chorus of cheers met his plan.

"Naomi should have been paying attention to the play." That came from Chris who followed up his statement with an "Oomph" as someone took offence at his criticism.

Chris, only a year older than her and most often the victim of her mood swings as the slowest brother, always held the least amount of sympathy for her. And yet, despite his words, he would stand first in line to kick the ass of anyone who ever intentionally hurt her.

On and on the bickering went, peppered with the occasional shove and slap.

When the noise level began to make, her already throbbing head, ache even worse, she lobbed the ice pack at her nearest brother with unerring accuracy, clocking him hard upside the head. Instant silence settled on the room as six pairs of eyes swiveled to look at her.

"If you're all done arguing, I'd like to go home now," she stated quietly. Her looming brothers and father all took a step back, her calm words a warning they knew all too well. She rose from the couch, her short and curvy, five foot four frame taut. The room spun and nausea made her stomach roil.

"Now, baby girl," her father began in a placating tone. "You should lie back down. The doc said you've got a concussion."

"Which is already healing," she interrupted. "Shifter blood, remember?" One of the advantages of owning Lycan blood was the ability to heal quicker than humans. Of course, quicker didn't mean instant, so while she waited, she'd still suffer some discomfort.

"Still," her father continued bravely. "The doctor said we should keep an eye on you, just in case you faint or something before your body has a chance to fully cure the problem."

Naomi crossed her arms over her chest, resisting an urge to sit before her trembling legs gave out. "Are you trying to tell me I can't go home?" She arched a brow and her father swallowed.

Chris rolled his eyes. "Oh, let her go. If she wants to cause a car accident and maybe kill some hapless pedestrian by being pig headed and driving herself home, then let her."

The heated glare she shot Chris's way made her head spin. Worse, her brother stuck his tongue out knowing she didn't feel well enough to make him hurt for it. "If I weren't a lady, I'd kick your scrawny little ass," she muttered. She ignored the snickers and the whispered, "Since when is she a lady," comment that followed her words, but only because of her throbbing head.

A sigh escaped her as her brother's truthful words battled her stubborn nature. Much as she hated giving in to their no driving order—well-intentioned or not—she wouldn't operate a motor vehicle if she could prove a danger to others. "Fine, so if I can't drive myself, then who is taking me home?"

Six pairs of eyes found the ceiling suddenly intensely interesting.

Irritation made her lips draw tight. "Oh, come on. Surely one of you idiots can handle my car?"

Kendrick cleared his throat before speaking. "Um, the last time Mitchell drove your car, you almost castrated him because he didn't shift it to your satisfaction. You told us never to touch your car again, or else."

Naomi blew out a breath. *Pussies.* How could they blame her for taking offence at the brutish manner with which they drove her baby? They'd deserved each, and every, smack. And then, they had the nerve to wonder why she wanted to get away from the shifters and their violence. They bloody well drove her to it.

"I am not staying here." Not with her mother due home within the hour from work. Once her mom walked through that door, Naomi would be lucky if she got to leave a bed within the next three days. The men in her family might fear their baby sister even as they coddled her, but everyone obeyed their mother. Nobody owned the balls not to.

The doorbell rang and as one, her family dove to answer, leaving her alone. Naomi shook her head. *Afraid of little old me? Good.*

Not interested in the caller, Naomi walked with ginger steps so as to not jostle her aching head into the kitchen to look for some alcohol. The Tylenol she'd taken, twelve pills so far, had done almost nothing for her pain. Banned from driving and lacking a chauffeur, she might as well get a little drunk, a plan forgotten as the snarls started from the front of the house.

"Now what?" she grumbled as she stalked toward the fracas, lancing pain rousing her temper.

A wall of brothers stood between her and the menacing growls of her daddy, which ran counterpoint to some unknown deeper rumble and a more feline yowl—both which sent shivers skating down her spine, and not the unpleasant kind.

A few well-placed elbows and she'd shoved her way to the front of the crowd to find her father facing off, nose to nose, with non-other than the behemoth from the lacrosse match. She'd have recognized him anywhere seeing as how not too many Kodiak bears chose to live near civilization. And damn, but up close like this he appeared even larger than expected, completely towering over her and wider than logic dictated a male should be.

Seven foot and a bit of bristling bear stood at her front door, and not just any bear, but one who'd injured her. No wonder her canine family acted so agitated. Actually, so was she for that matter and not just because of the ball she'd almost swallowed, her wolf started spinning in circles inside her head with excitement and Naomi didn't like it one freakn' bit. It didn't help that this close to the behemoth, awareness lit up all the nerves in her body, and an inhalation of his scent sent moist heat to her cleft. *Oh, like hell is this hulking bear my bloody mate.*

Squeezing herself between her father and number forty-four, she jabbed her finger into his chest. She might as well have poked a brick wall because the flesh of his chest didn't give one iota. On the other hand, that brief contact sent a sizzling bolt through her system.

Failed poke or not, it did, however, catch his attention. Brown eyes broke off their staring match with her father and rotated down to peer at her. He inhaled deep as he stared at her, increasing the tingle that ran through her body like an electric jolt. It fired up more than her cleft—it sparked her ire.

"What are you doing here?" she demanded rudely, clenching her fists at her side before she gave in to the urge to stroke the firm chest in front of her.

"I, um, wanted to see if you were okay and say I'm sorry you, um, got hurt." His halting words rumbled pleasantly over her skin. Naomi, unable to resist, sucked in a breath and found her senses flooded with a titillating whiff of soap, bear and male musk all of which sent her wolf into a tizzy.

Oh god, I need to get him out of here, pronto. "I'm fine. Bye." She waited, but as she feared, he didn't just turn around and leave.

"Um, that wasn't the only reason I came."

Flowers were suddenly thrust in her face, a wild bouquet of blooms that made her want to sneeze. She batted them to the side. She narrowed her eyes up at him and enjoyed the way it made him swallow. *He fears me. Good.* "What else do you want? Isn't it enough I've got two black eyes and a headache the size of Quebec?"

"I'm really sorry about that. I was kind of distracted." His brown eyes looked so pained that Naomi fought an urge to tell him it was okay—and throw herself in his arms. "Actually that's part of the other reason I'm here. See, I—uh—well, that is, I think we're mates." He stammered the words out and ruddy color flushed his cheeks.

Her greatest fear spoken aloud, panic gripped her and she lost her mind. "Over my dead fucking body we are. You've got a lot nerve coming here," she yelled, her shrill tone making her headache flare stronger. "As if I'd waste any of my time with a guy who can't even catch one little rubber ball. Now, go away and just forget about me."

"But—"

Naomi froze him with an icy glare at odds with her melting pussy. She fought to hold onto her anger, a feat harder than expected when confronted with almost seven towering feet of muscled male. His square craggy features should have turned her off with their obvious lack of gentle refinement, but instead she found herself intrigued by his square jaw, his crooked nose and his soft eyes framed by thick dark lashes. He kept his hair short in a military type brush cut that displayed the gold hoop in one of his ears.

As for his body, he stood too close for her to ogle it, but since the lacrosse game, she could imagine it—from his extremely wide shoulders dropping down to a tapered waist that led into thick muscled thighs and an ass of steel. *I wonder if his cock is as big as the rest of him.* Naomi bit her lip at the train of her thoughts. *I do no care what he looks like. This Neanderthal is not my mate.*

"I'm sorry. Do you have a hard time understanding English? I told you to leave." Her brusque tone made his eyes turn puppy dog sad and she wanted to smack her forehead on something hard—say like his delicious chest?

Snickers, which turned into outright laughter, erupted from behind the wall of flesh in front of her. Naomi couldn't help but crane sideways to see who found the untenable situation so amusing before she resorted to violence. *And my family knows how I hate it when that happens. Try to be a lady and no one listens. They'll start paying attention when my foot starts connecting with some soft spots.*

Her icy gaze caught the attention of yet another lacrosse player, and her wolf just about slobbered in excitement all over mind. *Oh, hell no.* As her gaze became caught by the eyes of dark haired number sixty-nine from the lacrosse match, she wanted to hurt something really bad because if she wasn't mistaken, the damned kitty cat in front of her—another testosterone pumped male—was also her mate. *Not two. Surely fate wouldn't be so cruel?* While not all that common, she knew mating could occur in pairs or more, she'd just never assumed it would happen to her. *No fair. I don't even want one. Why the hell do I suddenly have two on my doorstep?*

Irritation held over panic—barely. She focused her ire on the jerk who found the situation so hilarious. "I wouldn't laugh seeing how it was your poor aim that gave me my rainbow face and headache."

Actually, number sixty-nine's humor had dried up the moment their gazes caught, and if she weren't in such shock herself , she would have enjoyed his dropped jaw and the look of fear—and smoking desire—that crossed his face.

"Uh. Uh." Like a slack jawed idiot, the suave looking number sixty-nine couldn't even mutter a coherent sentence.

"Apparently you've gotten a ball to many in the head, too. Now if you don't want my foot to get shoved up your butt, because I am just about to lose my temper, then I'd suggest you get your asses out of here."

"But," the behemoth tried to interrupt.

"Go away," she screamed, meaning to follow up her panicky plea with action. Vertigo along with a blinding pain in her head, though, made her unable to do what she wanted—which closely resembled running away and escaping the sure mess these two men would surely try and make of her life. She only managed an "Ah, fuck," as her family and doctor's prediction came true. She succumbed—unwillingly—to unconsciousness.

Chapter Three

It had proved surprisingly easy to discover the identity of the injured female. Javier simply questioned a few staff members while Ethan glowered. In short order, they were handed the information along with wishes of "Good luck" and "Glad I'm not you."

Ethan paid the pitying looks no mind, too caught up in his own inner misery of how to approach the female slated as his mate. Javier, on the other hand, couldn't stop grinning. He just wished he dared tape the event because seeing his enormous friend reduced to a quivering mass of jelly provided great entertainment.

His theory that the upcoming meeting would prove interesting held—and made him wish for popcorn—as Ethan knocked on the door of the house where several sources assured them the female, named Naomi, would have been taken.

A crowd of large men—none as big as Ethan of course—answered. An older, grizzled male, eyed them up and down before barking, "You're the idiots who got my daughter hurt. You've got a lot of nerve showing up here."

Things degraded from that point with the younger males—brothers, Javier assumed—growling and jostling for position and challenge. Ethan didn't back down. While women might tie him in knots, especially the prospect of meeting his mate, violence he understood. Ethan stepped forward actually going toe to toe with the elder wolf.

Javier wondered if he should speak up. *Do I warn my friend against beating up the father of his intended or prepare to come to his aide?* Neither proved necessary as the rumbling of testosterone soaked males died down as someone shoved through their ranks. Javier couldn't see, but he could hear a melodious voice, threaded in steel, order his friend away, mate or not. The situation at that point became too comical and Javier couldn't hold back the guffaws, a laughter he almost choked on as an oval face garnished in multihued bruises and framed in long, brown hair peered around Ethan's body to glare at him. With that one extremely icy stare, Javier knew fear for the first time in his life.

His panther, on the other hand, yowled with excitement in his mind. *Oh fuck, no. She's my mate too.*

Horror engulfed him at the thought even as he couldn't help but drink in the sight of her from her flashing grey eyes, her rosebud and delectably full lips, to her curvy and heavily breasted frame. A surge of desire rushed through him, making his cock twitch even as his jaw dropped in disbelief. Words were spoken, but Javier, caught in a frozen moment of disbelief, barely registered them.

He snapped out of it when pandemonium erupted as with an indelicate "Ah, fuck", the female's eyes rolled up in her head and she collapsed. Too many pairs of hands reached out to grab her. As the biggest, Ethan won and he held his prize up high, growling a warning at Naomi's father and brothers as they jostled and shouted for him to give her back. Things promised to devolve quickly if common sense didn't prevail.

Javier shoved in front of his friend and faced off with the bristling group of males. He held up his hands, trying to school his features into something that would calm them down rather than set them off further. "Gentlemen, surely all this yelling and posturing isn't helping the young lady? And it's probably alarming the neighbors. Could we not adjourn inside?"

"I think you should all listen to the cat."

Where Javier's words had provoked only heated glares and growls, the delicate feminine voice from behind him sent the males confronting him scurrying. Trepidation sunk its claws into Javier as he wondered what could make such a tough looking bunch scatter. *A giantess, thought extinct sphinx, a deadly siren?* He turned and held himself ready to run—or defend himself. A pent up breath whooshed out of him as he regarded the petite woman with graying hair who eyed him up and down with interest.

"And you are?" she demanded in a tone that brooked no nonsense.

"Javier, ma'am," he announced thrusting out his hand. "Number sixty-nine for the Loup Garou lacrosse team."

Slim fingers gripped his firmly as she shook his hand. "And the big fellow holding my daughter?"

Ethan rumbled in answer. "Ethan, ma'am, number forty-four"

"You are responsible for her current injuries I assume?"

"Yes, ma'am. I'm awfully sorry. I was kind of distracted by your daughter."

Finely arched brows lifted. "Distracted? By Naomi?"

Ethan forged on ahead. "Yes, ma'am. I caught a glimpse of your daughter in the stands, and, well, she's my mate."

"Really?" The petite woman pursed her lips at that answer.

Javier thought about holding his tongue, but with a sigh he gave in, somehow knowing if he didn't this little woman would make him regret it later. "Um, sorry to interrupt, but I think I might also be her mate."

"What?" Ethan yelled. "You didn't tell me that when we were on our way over here."

Javier shrugged. "I didn't know until I set eyes on her. Trust me, I am just as unhappy about this as you are. I'm not meant for monogamy."

A cleared throat had Javier blushing as piercing gray eyes riveted him with disapproval. "I think we all need to go inside. *Now.*"

Javier didn't stand around arguing, and neither did Ethan who stomped inside holding the still unconscious Naomi in his bear paws. Strangely, Javier wanted a turn cuddling the lush—and feisty—female, a crazy urge that he tamped down. *If Ethan wants her, then Ethan can have her.* Maybe once his friend marked her, this urge to sniff her and lick her—even worse, mark her as his cat demanded—would cease.

He almost ran into Ethan's back when he stopped suddenly. He stepped around him at the prodding of one none too happy mother, and he found the reason in the form of a line of men, all with their arms crossed over their chests.

The elder one spoke. "What are you doing inviting them into our home after what they did to her face?"

The petite woman faced off with the grizzled male, her hands planted on her hips. "I'm sorry, Geoffrey, did you suddenly become lord of the manor while I was at work, and me, a simple maid who can't decide who comes into our home?"

The man who had to be Naomi's father almost blanched at the quiet words. One of the big lugs at his side actually cringed. "Now, Meredith, you know that's not what I meant."

Meredith, Naomi's mother, arched a brow. "Good, then I don't see the problem with inviting in our two future son-in-laws."

And with those glibly thrown words, pandemonium resumed.

* * * * *

Naomi's head throbbed, and the yelling going on around her didn't help, rather it added to her general malaise and irritation. What she did find comforting was the lap she found herself cuddled in. Strong arms held her close against a hard chest where a rapidly beating heart lulled her for a moment longer before sanity set in.

Whose freakn' lap am I on?

Somehow, she doubted they were related to her given the evident erection poking at her bottom and the fact her whole body tingled. *Oh no, one of them has got me.* Panic made her scramble to escape before she opened her eyes. She dove off the warm lap and didn't peer around with wild eyes until she found herself clear of bodies, nausea and pain weaving a dance in her body that made her want return to her unconscious state for a while longer. *Since when do I wish for the cowardly route?* She straightened her spine and took in the scene before her.

Out from the cocoon of the behemoth's arms, the noise seemed even louder and chaotic. On one side of the living room, her mother stood nose to nose with her father, who, in this rare instance, wasn't backing down on whatever they fought about. Three of her brothers stood around number sixty-nine, haranguing him as he held up his hands in a conciliatory manner. As

25

for number forty-four, he sat on the couch and ignored her two other glaring brothers to watch her.

"Enough." Silence descended as she planted her hands on her hips and regarded them all. Her head pounded fiercely, and all she wanted was to go home and lie down. Alone. "Why are these guys in our house?"

"Naomi, is that any way to treat your beaus?" Her mom's voice cut the silence and Naomi grimaced at her.

"They are not mine," she growled. "No matter what they seem to think." Or her own inner bitch whined.

"Stubborn chit," her mother chided. "You can't fight fate."

"Watch me." Naomi went to stride out of the room, but a wave of dizziness made her sway, not far, though, as a new pair of firm hands grabbed her and tugged her into a solid embrace.

Heat enveloped her and she held in a sigh as she looked up into the tanned face of the feline. "Let me go."

"Of course." Immediately the male she still only knew as number sixty-nine released her and stepped away, but not far. His dark eyes watched her, a smoldering fire in their depths.

"Darling, why don't you sit down?" Her mother's suggestion held more a tone of command, but Naomi fought it.

"No. I want to go home." Naomi cursed the plaintive note in her tone, but she couldn't help it. Too much was happening and with her head dancing to the tune of an out of key Mariachi band, she just wanted peace and quiet. She also needed time to plan how to evade her sudden and unwanted suitors. A grimace crossed her face as she realized her damned mother, with a stubborn tilt to her chin, already plotted against her, determined to force her—probably kicking and screaming—to her fate.

"You, the big one," her matriarch ordered. "Ethan, if I recall correctly. You will drive my daughter home. Javier." Her mother pointed to number sixty-nine "You will follow so once your big friend drops her off he has a ride home. As for you." Her mother swiveled to fix her with a glare. "Get some rest. I'll see you and your beaus tomorrow night for dinner. No argument." Naomi's lips tightened into a thin line. *Oh, there will be arguing, just not right now while I'm not in tip-top shape.* Judging by the stormy expressions on her father's and brothers faces, they'd also have plenty to say once she left.

Chris tossed her car keys to number forty-four, whose name, Ethan, seemed too docile for a man his size. One big mitt came up to catch her keys and she wanted to protest the giant beast couldn't touch her car, but given the choice between escape or more of her family's tough love, she chose possible injury to her car.

Of course, before she could escape, she found herself enveloped in too many hugs, not as tight as usual, her brothers and father, treating her gingerly. She thought she saw her mother speaking to Javier in between embraces, but before she could see what they conspired, Chris squeezed her tight with a whispered, "Brat, figures fate would think you need two men to keep you in line." Her head didn't ache enough for her not to stomp on his foot, his yelp of pain making her almost smile.

Hugs accomplished and with no time to change her mind, she found herself pressed between a pair of male bodies, her breath stolen by their sudden nearness while heat flashed through her.

They made it outside before it crossed her mind that her mother had just sent her home with strangers—and ones who'd caused her current, if accidental, injury in the first place. It occurred to her to march back inside and lambast her parents for poor decisions, but Ethan rumbled. "Which car is yours?" and she decided to hold onto that harangue for later.

Naomi wondered who'd driven her car over as she obviously hadn't and Francine didn't do manual transmissions. *Whoever brought it, they'd better have treated my baby right.* She peered around for her red Miata and saw it parked in front of a shining, silver Lexus.

"Are those your wheels?" She asked pointing at the sweet ride she dreamed of but couldn't yet afford.

"Mine, actually," Javier replied.

"Nice," she replied grudgingly. "Mine's the red one behind it. Hurt it and I will hurt you."

"Promise?" Javier teased with a smile that hit her right between the thighs.

When she would have stumbled on the last porch step, she instead found herself swept up into Ethan's arms.

Heat at his proximity flooded her and she struggled. "Put me down. I can walk."

"And I can carry you. Your point would be?"

"Caveman," she grumbled, wincing at the twinge in her head.

"Are you always this irritable?" asked the cat.

Naomi shot him a glare. "Gee, let me see. My friend dragged me to a lacrosse game, which, I might add, is not my idea of a good time in the first place, where some clumsy bear missed a ball causing me to get injured. That same bear and his alley cat then show up and try to claim me as their mate even though I don't want one. I think I've earned the right to be annoyed."

"I told you we should have brought more flowers," Ethan grumbled.

"Flowers?" She turned incredulous eyes up to Ethan's face, but he didn't meet her gaze as he opened the passenger door on her car and deposited her in with a gentleness that seemed at odds with the aggressive demeanor he'd displayed during the game.

He slammed the door shut instead of answering her and crossed over to the driver side. He leaned in and tugged the lever to send the driver seat as far back as it could go. Then, he inclined the back rest.

"Dude, maybe I should drive her car. You're kind of big for it." Naomi silently agreed with Javier, but at the same time found herself morbidly curious to see if the bear would fit.

"And maybe you should invest in a wheelchair, because I'm about to put you into one," was the behemoth's growled reply.

Naomi leaned her head back against the headrest and prayed for the nightmarish evening to end.

The suspension on her car sank alarmingly as the determined bear shifter sat in the seat and Naomi shuddered at the imagined damage his weight would cause. But, at this point, arguing would just delay the whole trip and she really, really wanted to get home. *Besides, I can always just send him the bill.*

"Where to?" he asked turning those chocolate eyes her way.

Naomi gave him the directions to her townhouse and then tried not to flinch as he turned the key in the ignition. Stu tended to hold the starter a tad long making it whine. However, the beast let go as soon as the engine caught. Car started, he hit the gas and shifted, his movements smooth as he displayed a gentleness with her baby that made her ease somewhat. However, a lack of worry over his chauffeur skills meant she had time now to notice just how much space he took up in the cab of her car—he almost sat in the back seat, for Pete's sake, he was so damned big. She couldn't ignore how his scent, a soap and musky male mix, permeated the close space. When his hand brushed her thigh as he shifted gears, she jumped as if burned, tucking her legs tight against the passenger door. A soft chuckle made her cheeks burn as she realized he'd caught her reaction.

Attraction to the behemoth confused her. He embodied nothing she appreciated in a male, and yet her body reacted as if she'd sucked back a whole bottle of Viagra for women. *I'm freakn' horny.*

The knowledge bothered her almost as much as her nagging headache. Sure, he sported a great body and a decent face; however, she prided herself on looking past a male's exterior to his insides for intelligence, manners and common interests. She never allowed her hormones to rule her, choosing boyfriends who met her strict criteria starting with them not belonging to any shifter caste. *And how boring has that been?* Her sarcastic conscious continued to snipe at her. *It's just because I haven't met the right one.* Her inner wolf yapped and made her gaze slide over to the behemoth whose big paw clutched at her steering wheel with white knuckles. *Stop that. He is not the man for me. He's a boneheaded jock, goddammit.* Her mental assertion didn't stop her inner wolf from snorting, her disgust evident.

They got half way to her house before Naomi frowned at the silence in the vehicle. *As my supposed mate, shouldn't he be trying harder to woo me? Or is he plotting?* She shouldn't care, but her wayward tongue always wagged before she thought.

"Why so quiet?" she asked rudely.

Brown eyes flicked over to catch hers for a second and Naomi sucked in a breath at the banked fire in their depths. "I'm not good with words. I thought it best, especially given your current state, that I not speak."

Naomi bit her lower lip at his admission. It was actually kind of nice, not that it helped his case. "Thanks. I think. Listen, I know you think we're mates or something, but I can assure you it's a mistake."

"You prefer Javier?" he growled.

His accusation made her blink. "No. I don't want to be mated with a shifter, any shifter."

That comment turned that melting gaze her way again. "But you are a shifter. Shifters mate. And I am not mistaken. You are mine."

The possessive claim made her shiver in a way that tightened her nipples. Pursing her lips, she ignored how it made her feel and forged ahead. "See, it's that kind of attitude that irritates me. My wolf is only a part of me, and while she might think you smell good and want to do nasty things to your body." He choked. "I want more out of a partner in life than hot, animal sex. I want a man who will support me."

"I have money," he interrupted.

"I wasn't done speaking," she snarled and he clamped his mouth tight. "It's not just about money. I also mean support in the sense that I can have an intelligent conversation with him. Own pretty things that won't get destroyed because some testosterone laden male has decided he needs to vent some steam indoors."

"You think I'm stupid?" Anger threaded his words and Naomi felt a moment's chagrin.

She ignored it. "Not stupid, exactly, but come on, you're an athlete, not an intellectual. Are you going to tell me your first instinct is to talk things over or use your fists?"

"I'm annoyed right now and yet I'm talking to you aren't I?" His sarcastic reply coincided with him pulling up in front of her house.

Without waiting for her reply, he exited the car, but before she could open her door, he appeared, and lifted her out.

"Would you put me down?" she exclaimed, exasperation coloring her tone.

"No. But, since you find me so offensive, perhaps you'd prefer Javier." Neanderthal A passed her to Neanderthal B while Naomi could only fume.

"Did I miss something?" Javier asked as he tightened his arms around her.

Naomi told her hip hopping tummy to take a hike before answering. "I was just explaining to your friend how neither of you will do as a mate. So please, put me down and be on your way."

"Are you challenging us?"

Ethan snorted as he fit her key into the lock and opened the door to her townhouse.

"No, I am stating a fact. Find some other gullible bitch to bite, fuck and fetch your slippers."

Javier's laughter washed over her in a warm wave she enjoyed way too much. Fuming that they wouldn't take her serious, she clamped her lips shut as the overgrown cat carried her into her home. He finally set her down on her couch, but then instead of leaving,

Ethan sat in the chair opposite her while Javier wandered off in the direction of the kitchen.

"Shouldn't you be leaving?" she asked with a pointed stare toward the door.

A shrug from massive shoulders answered her. "Make me."

"Ooh," she almost shrieked in exasperation. Only the pulsing of her painful head held her back. "Why are you both being so stubborn? Can't you tell you're not wanted?"

"My mama said the same thing to my dad when they first met," Ethan admitted. "Not liking her answer, he tossed her over his shoulder and kept her prisoner in a cave for two weeks, making love to her numerous times a day until she finally admitted she loved him, too," he added with a smug grin.

Naomi's jaw dropped and her throat worked soundlessly for a moment. "You wouldn't dare!" Her mouth said one thing, her pussy, drenching at his words, screamed another.

"Well, as you've mentioned a few times, I'm probably too dumb to know better. Although, don't worry, because of the lacrosse season, maybe I'll just handcuff you to a bed instead of finding a cave."

"My family won't stand for it!"

"Children, children," Javier chided returning to them holding two open beers, and one tall glass of juice. "Can't we all get along? After all, since our beasts have seen fit to join us in a ménage, we'll be together a long, long time."

"Over my dead body," she growled.

"Not dead, but gagged can definitely be arranged," Ethan grumbled.

"Hmm, a little kinky, but I'm not averse to the idea," Javier added.

Irritated, frustrated—and so fucking horny at the idea of them tying her down to have their wicked way—she took a swig of the juice, sudden thirst making her down the whole thing.

It didn't take long for wooziness to set in. She blinked as their image wavered. "You drugged me," she accused, trying to push herself up off the couch, but her body wouldn't obey.

"Your mother's orders," Javier explained. "You need to rest, but fear not, we will watch over you and make sure you come to no harm. Sleep, feisty one, and we'll sort things out when you feel better."

I am going to kill my mother. Naomi slumped over before she could tell Javier where he could shove his sorting out idea.

Chapter Four

"You drugged her?" Ethan bellowed the words as he surged from his seat, fists clenched.

Alarm crossed Javier's face and he held up his hands in a placating manner. "Calm down. It wasn't my idea, but her mother's. She handed me the pills along with the instructions to feed them to her with some juice to mask the taste."

"When the hell did she get the chance to give you drugs?"

"While Naomi's family was saying good bye, she slipped them to me."

"Why not just give them to her? Why con her into taking them?" Ethan wanted to smack his friend for pissing Naomi off even more.

"According to her mother, the only way to medicate her properly is by subterfuge. She'd already refused the medication from the doctor claiming she didn't want to be out of control."

"She is going to be so angry when she wakes up," he replied shaking his head, his expression surely woebegone. At least he could point the finger at Javier with a clear conscience and let his friend take the blame.

Ethan lowered his fists and moved to sit on the couch. He dragged Naomi's petite—and now quiet form—onto his lap. Despite her insults and the fact she currently looked like the loser in a boxing match, she fascinated him. Tiny—to him at least—and injured, yet she still stood up to him like she could take him in a fight. That took guts. In his experience, women bedded him for the thrill, but they never dared argue with him. Hell, he only needed to scowl to send them scurrying with shrieks of terror.

More fascinating, though, than her utter lack of fear toward him was her reaction to Javier. Women never rejected Javier, and the fact one slated as his mate did agitated his best friend—and amused the heck out of Ethan.

"What else did her mother tell you?" Ethan asked, looking for any advantage in his task of winning her over.

"That she'd call us later and give us pointers on wooing her daughter. Apparently, Naomi has something of a stubborn nature."

A snort escaped him. "I hadn't noticed."

Javier paced the living room as Ethan stroked Naomi's silky hair, unable to resist running his fingers through the long brown strands. "What are you thinking?"

"That fate is laughing at me."

A chuckle made Ethan's chest vibrate, causing Naomi's head to jiggle. He cradled her head in his big palm to prevent her from falling before replying. "She's certainly not what either of us expected, that's for sure."

Javier shot him a dark look. "No shit, Sherlock. I mean don't get me wrong, short and curvy works fine for me, but I always expected, if ever fate was cruel enough to curse me, she'd at least give me a woman who likes me."

"I'm sure she will in time. We took her by surprise, not to mention she's in pain. Besides, I kind of like that she's feisty. She'll need it to keep up with us."

Round eyes and an open mouth met his answer. "You, my friend, are insane. One ball too many to the head I think. I mean, not only does she not want you, shouldn't you be more pissed that it looks like she's meant for both of us?"

Ethan shrugged. "I'll admit, I never expected to share, but if fate says that's my lot, then at least it chose someone I could tolerate. And beat in a wrestling match if I need to. Besides, I'll only have to share if you bother to stick around to mark her."

"Oh, I'm staying, so you can forget about keeping her for yourself," Javier replied shooting him a dark look.

"What happened to I'm not meant for monogamy?" Ethan pitched his voice mockingly.

A sigh emerged from Javier's mouth before he slumped in the chair across from him. "I haven't thought that far ahead. It's hard to think at all with my damned cat yammering for me to bite her. Mayhap if you were to claim her first, the need for me to do so would vanish?"

The optimism in his friend's voice made him laugh again. "Sorry, no such luck I'm afraid. From everything I've ever heard, once you find the one, you're done for. The need to mark her, claim her, just gets stronger and stronger." Already the urge to take her rode Ethan hard. It didn't help that he held her cuddled on his lap, her sweet fragrance tickling his nose while her lush body pressed against his turgid cock.

"I don't suppose you'd care to explain the we-don't-have-a-choice aspect to Naomi?" Javier rejoined sarcastically.

"Why bother? She's bound and determined to fight her beast and in turn, her shifter nature. I say let her."

Incredulity marked Javier's expression. "Isn't that counterproductive to your, make that our, goal?"

"No, it is simple biology," Ethan explained. "She will eventually come to us. Keep in mind, the longer she denies the pull to mate, the harder the desire to claim us will ride her."

"That sounds kind of callous," Javier remarked. "I'm surprised. I expected more of you."

"You didn't let me explain what my plan was while she fought her nature. I plan to stay glued to her side, apart from practices and games, of course. I will get to know her, and in turn, she will come to know me. Befriend her, in other words, and if I'm lucky, perhaps she'll even come to love me. I know I'm already half way there." A romantic like his father, Ethan believed in love at first sight despite his more pragmatic friend's comments.

Javier snorted. "Gods, don't let the opposing team ever hear you yapping like a woman. For a giant bear, you're awfully sentimental."

A dark look shot Javier's way made his feline friend grin. Ethan growled. "You are lucky I am holding her, or I'd make you swallow your words."

"Down Smokey," Javier joked. "Actually, your plan is a good one. She is most definitely intriguing, and if we're going to spend the rest of our lives with her, then I guess becoming her friend before her lover is a good start. But I warn you, if she insists on sex, I will sacrifice myself for the greater good to please her."

"Whatever," Ethan scoffed. "You might be the oral master, but I will still always have the bigger cock."

And with that parting shot, Ethan stood with his precious burden and lumbered upstairs to find her bedroom.

* * * * *

Javier ended up following Ethan upstairs, unable to stay away from the lush female who'd somehow attracted him and his beast. It had occurred to him several times on the way over to simply drive away—and keep going until he snapped the tenebrous connection forming between him Naomi, and in a strange twist, Ethan.

Jaguars, the males at any rate, tended to spread their love, only rarely settling down, or so he'd been taught. His own father sired cubs on almost a half dozen females and never chose to mark any of them. Truthfully, Javier expected to follow the same path, already his conquests were numerous, although, unlike his father, he'd chosen to use protection to prevent conceptions. However, in the space of one night, instead of deciding which flavor he'd try next, he found himself irresistibly drawn to one curvy female with long, brown hair whose face he couldn't even guess at given the bruising and swelling, yet glimpses at pictures on her walls showed a striking woman. *One fated to be mine.*

But if he caved to his needs, he'd not only bury his prick in one sheath for the rest of his life, he'd also have to share her.

In the past, Javier had graciously shared his feminine conquests with his best friend, Ethan. A good guy at heart, his big friend's somewhat untamed appearance and shy demeanor made it hard for him to pick up women. Javier lost count of the threesomes they'd indulged in—where their hands and cocks stayed firmly pointed in the woman's direction only. It seemed fate enjoyed a quirky sense of humor, setting them up to both fall for the same girl, a girl who wanted neither.

However, my biggest fear is what if she does end up falling for me? Say I mark her and I end up straying? Apart from the damage Ethan would do to him if he hurt this woman, the thought of doing something so dishonorable made Javier ill. It was one thing to indulge in one-night stands where he and his partner went in with their eyes open, and no expectation of a tomorrow. It was a whole other thing to betray a woman he'd marked as his forever more.

Yet, even fear couldn't keep him from entering the room where Ethan deposited Naomi's unconscious form on the bed. He still felt kind of guilty about the whole drugging thing, but his orders had come straight from the mama wolf herself along with the tiny pill bottle. It would take a much braver cat to deny that matriarch anything. At least now, Naomi rested quietly, a state sure to change by morning.

Eying her, still fully dressed down to her shoes, Javier frowned. "We need to undress her," he stated.

"Like fuck. We are not going to take advantage of her while she sleeps."

Javier rolled his eyes as he scrounged through her drawers looking for sleepwear. He didn't find any silky negligées—*something I will have to rectify*—so he settled for a worn t-shirt and cotton shorts. Turing with the garments to face his friend, he found himself subjected to a fierce scowl. "Give me a little credit. I just meant to make her more comfortable, or do you really think she's going to enjoy waking up in jeans, a bra and shoes?"

Ethan's gaze dropped to her shape which he hadn't even tucked under the blankets. "Okay, you might have a point," he grudgingly admitted. "But no touching or I'll make you eat my fist."

A snort was Javier's reply. With two pairs of hands, they made quick work of divesting her of clothing, stripping her down to her white cotton panties.

A whistle emerged from his lips and despite the situation, his cock swelled.

"This is wrong," Ethan muttered in a thick voice as he stared at her rounded shape.

Javier could only silently agree as he too stared at Naomi's almost nude form. Her breasts were a heavy handful with large pink nipples that puckered as he watched. Her skin, smooth and creamy beckoned, as did her indented waist, flaring hips, and softly rounded tummy.

Shaking himself free of the stupor that gripped him as he stared dumbly at her body—*she's a woman like any other, nothing special*—he deftly dressed her, and with Ethan's aid, tucked her under the covers. He fought the insane urge to crawl in after her.

"Ready to go?" Javier asked a tad too brightly, eager to leave so he could get home and take care of the problem in his pants.

"I'm not going anywhere," Ethan rumbled. "She's helpless right now. If something were to happen, say, like, a fire or home invasion, she'd get hurt. I'm going to stick around."

The bear raised a valid point and gave them a plausible reason for them to not leave Naomi. Javier refused to examine the fact both of them didn't need to stay and play bodyguard. No way was he leaving Ethan alone with her. "I guess we're sleeping over then. In that case, I'm showering first," he announced, his rigid cock leading the way as he headed for the bathroom he found off the master bedroom.

"Jerk," Ethan muttered, his own need to fist himself probably even greater given he didn't indulge in sex as often.

Javier, though, showed him no sympathy, not when arousal gripped him so tight. Considering he hadn't yet bound himself to Naomi, he could have probably left and found a pair of accommodating thighs, but even thinking it made him feel dirty. Ashamed.

Better to take care of himself with his hand than question his sudden morals.

Of course, his evolving morals didn't mean he didn't jerk off to the image of the delectable Naomi, her face bruise free like the portrait he'd seen downstairs, and even better, on her knees eagerly begging for his cock.

Slowly, his hand slid back and forth across the smooth skin of his dick, the edge of his fist butting up against his pronounced head. He squeezed his hard length as he pumped, the water and soap making him slick and easy to stroke. Lifting one leg to prop it on the side of the tub, he allowed his other hand to cup his balls. Kneading them between his fingers, he stroked himself faster, the vivid image of Naomi bent over, her rounded ass presented to him, making him pant. He brushed his thumb over the head of his cock, spreading imaginary moisture over the tip before grabbing himself in a double grip and thrusting his hips back and forth into the tight tunnel his fingers formed. So easily could he imagine thrusting into her sweet pussy, his balls slapping against her, the curve of her buttocks butting into his groin. And when she came, would she scream or moan as her pussy convulsed around him? His cock liked either option and tightened as he reached the point of orgasm, the thought of her quivering release sending him over the edge.

I am in so much fucking trouble, he thought as he jetted his cream. Leaning his head against the tile of the shower, he let the intentionally frigid water cascade over his body.

Oh, Naomi, how am I going to keep my hands off you while Ethan and I teach you to want us too? At the thought of touching her, seeing her accepting him, naked with open arms, his shaft immediately hardened as if not sated at all.

Chapter Five

Naomi stretched as she woke with an exaggerated yawn in her own bed. *How the hell did I get here?* Recollection of the dirty trick the two men played on her the previous night made her sit up abruptly. The sheet fell away and she noticed her clothing of the previous eve gone, replaced with a t-shirt and shorts.

"Those dirty, rotten pigs," she cursed as she swung her legs out of bed and sat on the edge.

"You called?" A head topped with tousled hair poked out from around the door frame of the bathroom. Number sixty-nine's dark eyes twinkled and his lips curled in a sensual smile. Despite her irritation, her body flooded with warmth.

"You!" She pointed at him and shot him a dark glare.

He grinned wider. "What about me, darling?"

"I'm going to kick your balls so hard you're going to choke on them. How dare you drug me and then do despicable things to my body while I was unconscious?"

Stepping forward from the bathroom, he raised his arms in surrender and her eyes couldn't help drinking in the sight of him. *No one should look that delicious, especially in the morning,* was her disgruntled thought. Shirtless, Javier's tight and toned muscles beckoned. Encased in smooth, tanned skin, his muscular torso tapered down to lean hips where his jeans hung, partially unbuttoned and displayed a bulge that grew as she watched.

Unbidden heat flooded her cleft and her nipples shriveled so tight she could have drilled holes with them. She forced herself to swallow and look away before she did something stupid—say, like, licking her way down from his flat nipples to the dark vee of hair that disappeared into his pants.

"It would take a braver man than me to disobey your mother's orders. Besides, you needed the sleep," he added in a placating tone. Scowling, Naomi mentally planned a loud diatribe for her mother. "Let me ask you, how does your head feel now?"

His question derailed her for a second, and she paused to realize she actually felt pretty damned good— *but now I'm horny and it's all his friggin' fault.* She dove off the bed and stalked toward him, five foot four feet of annoyed woman craving coffee, a Danish, and him— naked inside her body. The first two she'd handle shortly, the third, she'd make him pay for. He stood his ground as she approached, the idiot.

"What did you do to me while I was out?" she growled as she patted her neck looking for a mating mark.

"Nothing. Contrary to your belief, snoring women with black and blue faces just don't do it for me."

His jibe hurt, but not as much as her foot when it connected with his undefended man parts. He ended up bent over, wheezing while Naomi smirked in satisfaction.

"That's for knocking me out. But, if I find out you did anything to me other than dress me, like cop a feel or take nudie pictures, I'm going hurt you a lot worse."

"Has anyone ever told you you're hot when you're mad?" said the man with an obvious death wish.

Only his speed saved him from her swinging fist as she screeched at him. "Go away. Can't you tell I'm not interested?"

"Liar." He threw that comment at her from the other side of her bed. "I can smell your arousal, sweetheart. And might I say, I can't wait to taste it."

The gush of wetness between her thighs made her groan in frustration as she fled to the bathroom and slammed the door shut. Chest heaving, she took a moment to compose herself. It didn't work so well, not when she couldn't get the image of his naked upper body out of her mind.

Needing a reality check, she braced her hands on the sink and peered at herself in the mirror. Most of the bruising on her visage had faded from dark purple to green and yellow. She still didn't look pretty, but at least her nose had returned to its normal size.

Yet, despite the way I look, I have two men clamoring to mate with me. Or should she revise that to only one? She hadn't seen or heard Ethan this morning. Perhaps, he'd wisely given up and left. Wishful thinking on her part probably because somehow she doubted she'd gotten so lucky. She got the impression number forty-four's giant body possessed even more stubborn genes than tanned sixty-nine.

Ignoring the fact a gorgeous man—that her inner bitch wanted to jump and gnaw on—roamed her bedroom, she stripped and jumped into the shower. As she washed her body, her hands lingered on her breasts and the apex of her thighs. She couldn't seem to stop, her body aroused and clamoring for any kind of touch, even her unsatisfying own.

It occurred to her that perhaps her out of proportion reaction might have come about because she'd not taken care of her needs in a while.

Maybe if I come, they won't affect me so much.

With that plan in mind, she cupped her breast, squeezing it, but she needed more stimulation than that—*a hot mouth sucking my nipple would feel so nice right about now.* She moaned as a mental image of Javier's dark head, bent as he tugged at her bud, made it shrivel and protrude. She rolled her hard nipple between her fingers while her other hand slid down her body to find her cleft. She leaned against the tile wall as she found her clit and stroked it.

Back and forth, she caressed herself, her hips gyrating as her wanton mind pictured Javier at her breast and Ethan on his knees, pleasuring her sex. Totally forbidden, so not what she wanted, but the erotic fantasy excited her like nothing she'd ever imagined and she rubbed herself with quick, slick strokes.

Would they take me one at a time, or would one thrust into my sex while the other fucked my mouth? No matter the answer, her cleft quivered at the thought of them penetrating her, filling her with their cocks and pounding until she orgasmed around their hard lengths. Stimulated in both mind and body, her climax approached and she let out a whimper as she increased the speed of her movements.

"You know, if you want some help in there, I'd be more than happy to oblige?" Javier's drawled words just outside the shower acted like a cold bucket of water. With a startled cry, Naomi snatched her hands from her pussy and breast as if scalded.

"Get out!" she screeched.

"Is that any way to treat one of your future mates?" he sighed. "And after I went through the trouble of warming a big, fluffy towel for you in the dryer?"

Incredulity made her peer around the plastic curtain. "You did what?"

A grin covered his face as he shook the towel at her. "Come on out while it's hot. I promise I won't look." He squeezed his eyes shut in exaggerated fashion and Naomi really thought about staying in the shower until he got the hint and left, but, of course, the water—in cahoots with the men apparently—turned cold. Standing there shivering, she reminded herself shifters didn't have the same hang ups about nudity as humans did—most of the time.

She dashed into the warm towel—*oh my god, that feels heavenly*—which he wrapped around her before sweeping her off her feet to carry her back to her room.

"What is it with you and your friend carrying me?"

"Exercise," he replied with a deadpan expression.

She snorted. "You are so full of shit and annoying. Did I forget to mention annoying?"

"But cute," he added, his lips tilting into a smile that made her stomach do hand stands.

He dropped her on the bed where she bounced with a squeal as she thrashed to hold onto her towel. She wasn't sure she entirely succeeded judging by the smoldering look in his eyes when she finally settled.

Tucking the edge of the towel securely around her body, her wet hair hanging down her back and dripping, she tried to regain her composure. "So where's the other Neanderthal, or is he the smart one and left?"

"Nope, dumber than a rock still," Ethan announced walking into her bedroom with a tray. Naomi's eyes widened as she saw the logo from her favorite coffee house on the Styrofoam cups and at least four Danishes.

"How did you know?" she asked as she dove on the steaming java. She took a burning sip and sighed happily.

"Your mother called to check on you. We actually had a great chat," Javier announced. He went to grab a lemon pastry and Naomi slapped his hand.

"Mine," she growled.

"But there are four of them. Surely you can share one?"

She shook her head. "I don't share, and I warn you, I bite."

"Promise?" Javier leered, his eyes twinkling.

Heat of a different kind burned her cheeks as she realized how her claim sounded. She ignored him and concentrated on her breakfast.

The mattress sank alarmingly as Ethan sat down beside her. She scooted over lest gravity drag her into the well he made. "Thanks for breakfast," she muttered through a mouthful of cherry Danish.

"My pleasure," he rumbled. "You're looking a lot better today."

"No thanks to you," she replied, shooting him a dark look. She almost felt bad at his chagrinned look—but got over it quickly when she reminded herself of the way they were attempting to take over her life. While she devoured her breakfast, begrudgingly letting the last Danish go because to eat it would have probably caused her to explode, Javier left. He returned with his upper body clothed. A shame.

"So what else did my mother tell you?" she asked, leaning back to suck on her coffee.

"That you were a colicky baby, hate the color pink, love your car, and that you're more stubborn than a mule," Ethan supplied.

"She would," Naomi grumbled darkly. "Did she also tell you I don't want to hook up with a shifter for the rest of my life? I want peace and quiet, not constant chaos."

"Yes, she mentioned something about a harebrained scheme involving marrying a human. Personally, I think you have way too much passion for a human male. Hell, from what I've seen, I'm not sure two shifters will be enough." Javier waggled his brows and leered comically.

Ignoring how cute this rendered him, she concentrated on his annoying—totally untrue—observation and used it to jump start her anger. She sprang up on her bed, only belatedly remembering she wore a towel, which plummeted leaving her naked. Ire, though, made her stand tall and wave her coffee at him. "I am a delicate, misunderstood flower, goddammit," she yelled. "Why does no one see that?"

Javier's eyes glazed over as he stared at her. "Delicate," he murmured. "Yes, certain parts of you certainly are."

A hand tickled up the back of her bare thigh, close to her core, which pulsed with heat and moisture. "Nice view," Ethan added.

Naomi, coming to her senses, realized the spectacle she presented and hopped off the bed with a bellowed. "Out. I need to get dressed." *And a way to get myself off before I embarrass myself completely.*

They complied, but not before Javier said, "We'll be just outside in case you want any help finishing what you started in the shower." Her inarticulate yell went well with the cordless phone she threw at him. They slid out into the hall and swung the door shut before it could hit them, and her poor phone hit the portal with an ominous crack. *Great, now I need a new phone.*

Panting, and not only out of irritation, she still managed to catch due to her damned wolf hearing Ethan's whispered, "What happened in the shower?"

Banging her head on the wall a few times, wincing as it brought back some of her pain, she wondered what she'd done to deserve this. Her inner wolf just howled in frustration and asked why she was so determined to act stubborn.

I don't want to mate with those two, chest-thumping shifters. I don't want to screw, at the same time, those two yummy shifters. I don't want to lick every inch of those two deliciously sculpted shifters. I don't…

Failing miserably with her inner pep talk, she took her time getting dressed, blow drying her hair and itemizing the reasons why her pair of jocks should look elsewhere for a mate. Unfortunately, her body kept coming up with its own list: they had wicked bodies, handsome faces, senses of humor, chivalrous tendencies. *And, they're also domineering, pig headed, probably violent and so obviously chaotic.*

Battle armor in place, rejection speech prepared, she sailed downstairs to give them a piece of her mind, only to discover they'd already left. She found a pair of notes in their place.

Naomi,

I had to leave for lacrosse practice. I'll see you later today. Yours, Ethan

Short and to the point, yet the claim he'd see her later made her flush. She read the second note.

Dearest Naomi,

Holding you in our arms last night, while you slept, was pure heaven. The glimpse we were blessed with of your delectable body? Absolute torture knowing we couldn't touch you and please you as you so rightly deserve.

We can only hope you'll think of us today, my face buried between your thighs, lapping at your sweet core as my friend takes care of your beautiful breasts. If you need to stroke yourself during our absence, please think of us and the pleasure we'll soon have plowing your body and making you scream in ecstasy.

Until I kiss you later, Javier.

The note should have disgusted her, annoyed her or at the very least ended up crumpled into a ball and tossed; however, nothing in the last twenty-four hours was going as expected. Instead of getting worked up at his dirty and presumptuous words, her knees trembled, her sex flooded with moisture, and a quiver ran through her body.

She just thanked god they weren't around or she just might have asked them to act out the scenes in the note—more than once.

Chapter Six

Ethan hated leaving Naomi without even saying goodbye, but Javier made sense when he said she needed space to come to grips with the recent events—and time to miss them. Ethan wrote his note and then almost shoved it up Javier's butt when he read his friend's. But then, he'd realized part of her getting to know him included realizing he didn't have the same flowery way with words Javier did. And, as his conscience reminded him, she hadn't yet fallen prey to Javier's charm, so perhaps his straight to the point methods would appeal. Or so he hoped.

Once at the sports complex, he couldn't concentrate on lacrosse practice. However, even at his worst, he still shone, catching and flinging the ball with speed and precision. He skipped the locker room after their two hour drills to hit the gym. He found comfort in the mind numbing sameness of exercise.

Thankfully, the weight room was virtually empty and his dark look had hurried out the few patrons. As he lifted weights and did his cardio, he indulged in thinking about Naomi, which, of course, brought about a hard-on of epic proportions and just aggravated his blue balls. Like Javier, he'd spent some time in the shower, jerking off, numerous times, not that it helped. He only had to think of Naomi to harden again.

It's not my fault. She's too damned hot.

Today he'd gotten a glimpse of the beauty he recalled from his first mesmerizing glimpse, which combined with his heated memory of her body spelled trouble with a capital T. He wanted her so freakn' bad, and not just because of the mating urge. That might have started the snowball rolling, but the more he heard her speak and the more she revealed of her stubborn, feisty nature, the more he simply wanted her.

Ethan didn't care for meek and submissive women. He abhorred those that feared him, especially since his code of honor dictated he'd never hurt one. Naomi appeared fearless and possessed a fascinating mind.

Unfortunately, the very things he admired about her meant he'd suffer an even harder battle trying to win her over. What did he, a muscle bound jock—with a university degree, so at least dumb didn't apply—have to offer her? He'd listened with dejection the previous evening on the phone as Naomi's mother detailed the things they had going against them. One, they were shifters. Two, they didn't mind violence and were damned good at inflicting it. Three, they had minds of their own. Four...

In other words, pretty much everything about them clashed with Naomi's list of requirements. However, as Meredith reassured them, Naomi just thought she wanted some meek and mild human. It was up to Javier and Ethan to show her why life with them would prove more fulfilling. *Somehow, I don't think showing her my giant cock will sway her mind.*

The only consolation in the whole fiasco was Javier didn't seem to enjoy any better luck. Naomi had clearly shown simple flattery and suave looks wouldn't make her melt.

Thankfully, Ethan didn't mind sharing with his best friend. They'd done almost everything together since their time at university, almost eleven years now, but while he didn't mind being part of a three-way, mating bond, he really hoped Naomi wouldn't shun him in favor of his slicker friend. Javier always knew the right things to say and do with a woman.

Somehow, between the two of them, they needed to convince her to give them a chance. To work together as a team to seduce and enthrall their spicy little wolf.

I need to woo her. Now if only he knew how. He'd done well with the Danishes this morning, a hint her mother had tossed his way when she'd called again this morning for an update. He hoped for even more clues to aid him in winning his woman when they met up with her family for dinner tonight.

He also figured he'd have to prove himself to Naomi's obviously overprotective father and brothers, but he'd jump over that hurdle when he hit it. One important thing he'd learned was no flowers, or chocolate, or any other things most women expected. Naomi didn't care for those trite offerings, but wandering through her home— almost austere in its decoration—he'd noticed one well-dusted curio cabinet filled with butterflies. Almost a dozen of them made of glass and so fragile he didn't dare even think of touching one.

But at least they'd given him an idea.

I might not have the words, but by damn, I'll make her like me.

* * * * *

Naomi didn't want to attribute her bad temper to the fact she hadn't seen hide or hair all day of the two idiots whom her wolf wanted to take a bite out of. However, telling herself she didn't care as she cleaned her house in a frenzy, while pretending she was happier with them gone, just agitated her even more.

When her phone rang while she stripped and made her bed—trying to erase the delicious scent of them lingering on the sheets—she needed to race downstairs, her upstairs phone having met the door in a fatal accident earlier that morning during her fit.

Diving onto the shrilly, ringing phone, she answered breathlessly. "Hello."

"Oh my god, did I, like, interrupt you having *sex*?" Francine's voice started out loud and tapered to an exaggerated whisper.

"What? No, I'm not having sex. Why the hell would you think that?" Naomi replied in disgust—mostly because her body kept begging to have sex—as she flopped on the couch.

"Well, I heard from my mother, who heard from your mother, that apparently you found your two mates. Or they found you. Lucky bitch. And lacrosse players, too. I knew it!"

"You know nothing," grumbled Naomi. "They might think they're my mates, but I am not binding myself to a pair of dumb jocks." With stupidly hot bodies and quirky smiles she refused to think of. "Oh, and thanks for sticking around last night to make sure I was alright."

"Ha. I'd have to be insane to opt for a ringside seat to your brothers brawling. Although, had I known hunky and hunkier were going to show up and start some fireworks, I might have thrown on a hockey helmet and stayed for the show."

"You are such a bitch," Naomi groaned. "Of all the friends in the world, I just had to end up with a sarcastic, smart ass—"

"Don't forget superhot and horny".

"—one."

Laughter poured from the receiver and Naomi pulled it from her ear and glared at it. When it died off to the occasional giggle, she brought it back to her head. "This is not funny, Francine. Did you know they drugged me and then cuddled me all night long?"

"Oh, the jerks. That's just awful. I'd kill them too if all they did was snuggle me instead of making me scream in orgasm. Yes! Yes! Oh, baby." Francine went in a paroxysm of fake climaxes that made Naomi seriously debate trading her in. Best friend since kindergarten or not, the situation was anything but amusing.

"Francine! This is serious. What am I going to do?" Naomi practically whined. *You could ride them until the cows come home,* her insidious mind interjected with a snicker. "I don't want to get mated with them."

A loud sigh preceded Francine's answer. "Wow, you are so unnatural for a shifter sometimes, Naomi. I would just love it if I found my stupid mate and here you've got two you don't' want. Care to throw one my way?"

"I thought my brother Mitchell was your one and only," Naomi teased.

"Don't talk to me about your brother, mister I-think-of-you-as-a-sister. My wolf knows it, I bet his wolf knows it, but the idiotic man runs the other way whenever I so much as smile his way. Now stop trying to change the topic. We were talking about those hunky men who want to get into your uptight pants."

"I am not uptight, just selective."

"Did it ever occur to you to expand your horizons? Maybe these guys are like closet geeks who get turned on by math like you do. Have you even bothered to check and see if they discourse in a civilized fashion instead of fist fighting at the first cross eyed look thrown their way?"

Naomi snorted. "You did see them play last night, right? We're talking about the behemoth, the guy who sent some of those players home crying to their mamas."

"Okay, so maybe the bear might be a tad rough, but hey, I bet he's a wild ride in bed." Francine yahooed and made slapping sounds while Naomi sighed and rolled her eyes unseen. Francine didn't have a serious bone in her body and seriously needed to get laid. "What about number sixty-nine?" Francine continued. "He seems like the civilized sort."

"I've heard he beds so many women he owns shares in Trojan." Francine's mirth made Naomi smile—grudgingly. "Anyway, even if they are nice guys, I don't want to just let them mark me and own me just because my wolf is aching to take a bite. I mean, we're talking for life. What if they're like my dad and leave their socks everywhere?"

"Only you would think that's a sin beyond compare. What if they can cook?" Francine countered.

"What if they like country music?"

"Teach them to love techno by stripping to it."

"What if they leave the toilet seat up?"

"They've got some electronic doohickey to take care of that problem, so stop coming up with excuses. Give them a chance. Get to know them. You know, you might be surprised."

"And my family will learn to act civilized instead of rampaging roughshod like animals. Yeah right. Anyway, I better get going. Mom's expecting me for dinner and given how I left last night, I can just imagine the state my brothers will be in. I'll give your love to Mitchell," Naomi sang, making kissy noises.

"Skank. I hate you," Francine replied with a giggle before hanging up.

Wearing a grin of her own, Naomi placed the phone back on the charger and surveyed her place. The fresh scent of lemon Lysol permeated the air, erasing the delectable aroma of her want-to-be-suitors. Now if only she could scrub her mind and body to remove the erotic taint they'd left on her.

A check of the time showed her running late for dinner at her parents. Giving herself a quick wash first, she changed into some well-worn jeans and a blouse. A light brush of her hair, a thin sheen of lip gloss and she headed over to her parent's house. It crossed her mind to wonder if the guys would have the nerve to show up, her mother had invited them after all, but doubtful given her cold attitude toward them. And besides, who would be nuts enough to volunteer for dinner with her family?

Apparently, dumb and dumber were. Upon seeing the Lexus parked at the curb of her parent's house, a myriad of emotions claimed her.

Anticipation—which she squashed. Irritation—which she would soon vent. Pure, panty wetting arousal—she didn't dare give into.

Stalking up the steps, she slammed the door open and discovered a tense silence. Javier and Ethan, perfectly at ease, sat on one couch, while, across from them, sitting and standing in various strained poses were her five brothers and father. She especially enjoyed their pointed glares.

Ignoring the smiles and scowls tossed her way by both parties, she stomped into the kitchen, looking for her mother.

"What are they doing here?" she growled.

Mama didn't even look at her as she pulled a gigantic roast from the oven. "Whatever happened to hello, nice to see you, or do manners no longer matter to you now that you've moved out?"

Swallowing a sigh of impatience, Naomi pecked her mother on a cheek with a brusque. "Hi mom"

"See, that wasn't so hard. As for your question, I told them to come for dinner yesterday, or were you not paying attention?"

"I didn't think they'd actually show up. They left this morning and I thought they were gone for good. Which reminds me, why the hell did you tell them to drug me? They could have been murdering rapists and you gave them permission to incapacitate me!" Naomi's tone got higher and higher as her pent up frustration vented.

"Watch your tone with me, young lady. I know you and your penchant for making mountains out of molehills. Your body needed to rest. I made sure you got it, and look at you, already almost healed. But do I get any thanks for being a caring parent? Oh no, I get yelled at." Her mom turned to face her, her hands flinging upward and matching her facial expression of 'Why me?'

Naomi snorted. "That guilt trip speech might work on dad and the boys, but don't forget I learned from you."

Her mother dropped the pretense and grinned. "Just keeping you in practice. Now as to your beaus, what do you think of them?"

"You tell me. Apparently, you've spoken with them more than I have." Naomi snagged a roll out of the wicker basket and nibbled on it as she perched on a stool.

"Well, that Javier, he's definitely a charmer. You should see the flowers he brought me. I get the impression he's a little shocked by his meeting you."

"Shock or not, that didn't stop him from trying to get a piece this morning," Naomi related with a blush. "The man's a walking sex ad and he knows it."

"Oh, so you're not immune to his charm?" Her mother's bright eyes missed nothing.

"Horny doesn't mean I'm going to tie myself to him. He's a bloody jock, for god's sake. And a womanizer. That doesn't spell happily ever after if you ask me."

"Your father was quite the lady's man before I came into his life. He chased and bedded anything in a skirt. But that all changed once he met me. It will happen with Javier too. You'll see. The mating bond will keep him true," her mother assured. "If not, then he'll learn the mistake of his ways." Her mother held up the carving knife with an evil glint in her eye.

Naomi choked on her bread. "Mom!"

As if she hadn't clued in to the fact she'd just promised bloody violence, her mother continued blithely on as she sliced the roast. "That Ethan, what a polite boy. A little bit shy, but so sweet. I get the impression he's already quite smitten with you."

"The man is a beast. Have you seen the size of his hands? He'd probably break every goddamned thing I own."

"I don't think you're giving him enough credit," her mother intoned, carrying the carved roast on a platter to the dining room while Naomi followed, her own hands full with a basket of buns and a dish of butter. "I saw how gentle he treated you yesterday when you fainted."

"The whole thing is moot anyway. I don't want shifter mates. I want a nice quiet human who won't require me to remodel the house every few months. You, them and a whole army of believers in fate won't convince me to join with them. I have no intention of living in a war zone and needing to buy crazy glue by the case."

"And you are deluding yourself if you think you can escape your destiny," her mother snorted before bellowing, "Dinner!" Small woman, big lungs, Naomi cringed as her mother's bellow right beside her made her ears ring.

A herd of men stampeded into the dining room, still jostling for position even after all these years. Only two chairs were never fought over—mama would kill them if they even dared touch the ones at the foot and head of the table. As if preplanned, Naomi ended up situated between Javier and Ethan. The large table had no trouble accommodating them all. Actually, it could have handled more, which was why she ended up with all her brothers across from her, still scowling.

For some reason, their attitude irritated her. She knew her reasons for not wanting Javier and Ethan here. What the hell was their problem?

"What's got your undies in a wedgie?" she asked as she heaped her plate high with food—mama's cooking was to die for.

"They shouldn't be here," Derrick grumbled with a dark glare.

"And we hear they spent the night at your house," Mitchell added on a growl.

"I assure you, your sister's virtue remains intact. We simply ensured she didn't' come to any ill while incapacitated" Javier replied before she could.

"I am perfectly capable of taking care of myself," Naomi added with an elbow in Javier's ribs.

"You were unconscious and required protecting," Ethan rumbled.

"No thanks to either of you and your sleeping cocktail."

"They drugged you!" Chris, her usually antagonistic brother, stood up from the table his fists clenched.

"Oh, sit down," her mother ordered. "I told them to dose her because, knowing your sister, she would have cleaned her house top to bottom instead of getting the sleep she required."

Chris sat down, but his eyes shot daggers, which went well with the lasers from her dad, the death wish from Maverick…Dammit, and they all wondered why she wanted to stay away from shifters.

She pretended not to see any of them and went to work on her food. Trust her mother to not let sleeping wolves—bears and jaguars—sleep.

"So Ethan, I heard through the grapevine you have a university degree. What did you study in?" her mother asked. Naomi almost choked. *The behemoth went to school? Probably a token degree received through an athletic scholarship.*

"Architecture, ma'am. When lacrosse season is out and before hockey season starts, I do freelance work for a few corporations."

She couldn't help the look of incredulity she shot his way. Educated wasn't something she would have accredited him with. Not that it changed her mind about him. He still remained a big, hulking bear.

Her mother beamed at him. "Call me, Meredith. After all, we're almost family."

63

"Mom!" Naomi shouted almost choking again on her food. "Would you stop that? I am not getting hitched with them."

Pretending she hadn't heard Naomi's outburst, her mother turned to Javier. "What about you? What's your degree in?"

Naomi, despite her claim of disinterest, stopped chewing to hear what he had to say.

"I studied at the same university as Ethan. Their lacrosse team is where we met and became friends. I've got a degree in computer engineering. In the off season, I freelance writing software for two large dot com companies."

An urge to bang her head on the table gripped her. Why did the jocks have to break the mold and prove they owned brains? Not that it changed anything, but it did make it harder for her to hold on to her reasons not to give in to temptation.

The rest of dinner passed with most of the conversation held by her mother and Naomi's suitors. When the talk revolved around to lacrosse and hockey, the male half of her family unbent enough to join in, their love of sports thawing them somewhat.

They weren't the only ones succumbing to warmth, caught between the two of them, Naomi found herself much too conscience of them; the brush of their thighs against hers, the heat of their bodies radiating from them and warming her skin. As if sensing her diverted attention, Ethan's heavy hand dropped onto her thigh, a huge paw that sent scorching heat straight through the fabric of her jeans to her skin below. He squeezed her thigh and Naomi knew she should shove it off, but she feared antagonizing her simmering brothers. Besides, she couldn't fight any longer the arousal which flooded her as if anxious to make up for the way she'd dammed its presence during dinner.

As if her growing awareness of Ethan weren't enough, Javier decided to join the mix, his own tanned hand sliding up and down her upper thigh, brushing so close to the apex of her thighs that she gritted her teeth when he kept missing it.

Desire spiraled inside of her, making her nipples harden and her breathing come quicker. Her unwilling erotic response, however, didn't pass by unnoticed. With a roar of, "That's our baby sister!" her brothers jumped up from the table as her mother shouted, "If you're going to fight at least take it to the living room."

To give Javier and Ethan credit, they stood up with their hands raised in a conciliatory gesture. However, to Naomi's mortification, her Lycan brothers could still smell her arousal and showed them no quarter. Dishes went flying along with fists. Grunts and thumps filled the air as a free for all brawl broke out. It amused, and at the same time annoyed, Naomi to see Ethan plant himself as a wall in front of her, protecting her from the violence with his own body. She almost jabbed him in the kidney for his attempt at chivalry, especially since he'd caused half the current problem. Harming him from behind, though, went against the grain.

Naomi's mother, used to these kinds of outburst, just calmly grabbed what she could and carried it to the kitchen. Naomi stalked after her snarling, "And this is why I want a normal human male." Her mother could only shrug in reply.

To the sound of crashing dishes and yelling, Naomi left without saying goodbye to anybody and jumped in her car. Taking off with a squeal of tires, she headed for home. *I should count my lucky stars they all reminded me why sleeping with them, horny or not, is a bad idea.*

Of course, her soaking cleft didn't agree. *Too freakn' bad.*

She slammed into her house, her body taut with tension. Unable to sit still, she grabbed her feather duster and started to clean her spotless home.

It shouldn't have surprised her to hear the doorbell a short while later. She'd actually expected it, but that didn't mean she answered. Humming to herself, she ignored it as she dusted fiercely.

A pounding on the door made her frown. If they dented her door—lovingly refinished a candy apple red with an antique knocker she'd hand polished—she'd dent them.

"Naomi, open the door," Ethan shouted.

"Go away," she hollered back.

"Please, let me apologize first." Ethan sounded so crushed, she ended up biting her lip, the sharp pain preventing her from caving to his demand.

"Let me try," she heard Javier mutter. "Sweetheart, we are so terribly sorry dinner degenerated into chaos. Your mother explained to us how much you dislike it when that happens. There is no excuse for our behavior. What if we promise it won't happen again?"

"Don't worry," she yelled back. "It won't happen again, because I want nothing to do with you. Now go away and leave me alone."

Instead of departing, whispering sounded; however, try as she might, she couldn't make out their words. Despite herself, she edged closer, straining to hear. A hairsbreadth from the door's surface and she still couldn't make out their words even though they still muttered. Annoyed, she crossed her arms over her chest because she drew the line at pressing her ear against the door—barely.

"We have a proposition," Javier announced all of a sudden, startling her. "Give us each a good night kiss, and we'll go away without further ado."

Naomi snorted. "Or how about I just ignore you both and you go away anyway?"

"Please, Naomi. I'll get on my knees and beg you if you'll just open the door and let me say I'm sorry."

It was Ethan's plea along with the knowledge she held the power to bring a behemoth like that to his knees and plead that made her unlock the door and swing it open. She ignored her snickering mind which whispered, *'Liar, You just want a taste',* while her damp cleft screamed, *'Let them in—right into your pants.'*

Two pairs of eyes locked onto her as she stood framed in the doorway. She held up a finger. "One kiss and you'll leave?"

Both of them slapped their hands over their hearts. "Promise. We are men of our words," Javier added.

"Fine. Let's get this over with so I can mop my kitchen floor. Who's first?"

"Such enthusiasm. You're killing me," Javier muttered as he placed his hands on her waist and drew her forward.

A fluttering sensation started in her stomach as she stared up at him, her gaze fixated on his full lips, which descended with maddening slowness toward her mouth. When he finally touched her lips, her breath hitched, the sensual slide of his mouth over hers driving her crazy. He increased the pressure, the tip of his tongue probing the seam of her lips, which she kept firmly clamped—barely. He didn't pull away at her refusal to comply, but instead grasped her lower lip with his and sucked it. Naomi couldn't help the low groan that slid from her.

With a wet tug, he pulled back, releasing her mouth. Naomi opened her eyes, her lids heavy with burgeoning passion. Javier's lips tilted into a smile. "Again, accept my apology for the dinner fiasco. You have my word, it won't happen again." He brushed her lips once more, a feather light touch, before he drew away with a whispered, "Good night, sweetheart."

Javier's hands slid from her waist with slow reluctance, but before she could mourn their loss on her body, thick paws took their place and turned her. Craning her neck, she peered up at Ethan, wondering how on earth she'd kiss him when he still stretched so far above her. He took care of the problem by lifting her until her mouth came level with his, and yet, he didn't immediately kiss her.

"No matter what, next time your brothers want to vent, I'll walk away. Anything to make you happy," he whispered against her lips before slanting his mouth over hers, his strength evident yet at the same time, restrained and gentle. Already warmed up by Javier's kiss, she sighed against Ethan's mouth and that gave him the opening needed to insinuate his tongue. At the touch of his tongue against hers, arousal swept through her body and made her shudder. Her hands crept up and slid around his neck as she opened wider, letting him plunder the depths of her mouth. It proved a good thing he held her up because Naomi felt absolutely boneless in his hands, her good intentions and ability to even remember her own name destroyed by two powerful kisses.

When Ethan dragged his mouth from hers and set her down, leaning her against the doorjamb, she opened glazed eyes to watch in befuddled confusion as he stepped away from her. "Good night," he rumbled in a voice none too steady. Then he and Javier walked away.

They're actually leaving? As if sensing her incredulity, the two males stopped just before their car and turned to wave.

"See you tomorrow," Ethan growled, his eyes bright and his jaw tight.

"Dream of us," Javier tossed with a grin.

Then, they left taking their delectable touch and sensual promise with them.

Naomi almost cried. Despite her general dislike of what they represented, she still wanted their damned bodies. Her desire pissed her off and the fact she couldn't have them irritated her even more. *I can't believe they walked away after one kiss. They had to know how horny I was. Still am.* And yet, they'd kept their promise, the jerks.

Her kitchen floor bore the brunt of her displeasure and emerged gleaming. Her pussy on the other hand, no matter how many times she tried to polish it, refused to stay satisfied.

Chapter Seven

At work the next day, Naomi found it exceedingly difficult to concentrate. She'd spent a sleepless night, squirming and horny. She'd tried masturbating, but to no avail. Five fingers couldn't satisfy her, not when she craved a man between her thighs—make that two men.

Diving into her work, she let the numbers on the receipts and ledgers before her suck her into a world she understood where the solutions to questions made sense. Followed a set of rules that never wavered. Where a relationship equaled one man and one woman, two people, not three, like the spot between her legs claimed.

Slowly, the columns of figures settled her for the first time in days. An affinity for mathematics growing up had led her into a career in accounting, most especially for other 'special' people like her. Given the longevity of shifters and convoluted family trees—because not all species believed in a monogamous paring for life—she'd acquired an extensive clientele.

A few hours into her perusal of a particular account, where an uncle had retained guardianship of his nephews and their trust fund, she noticed some claimed expenses and receipts not adding up. Brow wrinkled, she re-added the numbers several times but couldn't get them to reconcile which meant, most likely, a misappropriation of funds by the uncle, an unfortunately all too common crime in the case of orphans.

And not something she'd tolerate.

She fired an email off to the attorney in charge of the estate recommending an audit and a halt to funds while they investigated the matter. *That will teach the uncle to steal from those children.*

The noon hour arrived, but before Naomi could tell her secretary, Josie, to order her a sandwich, Josie peeked her head around the door. In a whisper that she might as well have shouted she said, "Oh my god, the two hottest guys ever have just walked in and want to take you to lunch."

No names were needed for her to know who'd shown up. Excitement fluttered in Naomi's breast and dampened her panties while her inner bitch yipped in anticipation. She snapped the pencil she held in half. "Tell them I'm working."

Josie's mouth rounded into an 'O' of surprise. "Seriously? I did tell you they were like totally delicious, right?"

"Not interested."

Shaking her head, Josie shut the door. Less than a minute later, it reopened and both Javier and Ethan strode in as if they owned the place. Naomi just about went cross eyed at the sight of them. *Josie wasn't kidding when she called them hot.*

Naomi had seen them in lacrosse gear looking mouthwatering fit and agile. She'd seen them in regular clothes, like jeans and t-shirts, appearing yummy enough to strip. But dressed in a suit? Dear lord, talk about scrumptious and cruel at the same time. Kind of like the cheesecake dribbled in caramel sauce she knew she shouldn't want or eat, but craved anyway.

The boys looked like they stepped off the pages of GQ, their suits obviously not bought off the rack, not given the way they hugged their bodies and outlined their broad shoulders. Ethan's brown eyes crinkled in amusement at her slack-jawed amazement. She wondered if they'd noticed if she dumped her bottle of water over her head.

Javier perched himself on her desk, invading her space with his tantalizing scent. "Hello, sweetheart. You are looking beautiful today."

The last traces of her unfortunate close encounter with the lacrosse ball had disappeared overnight. "I'm busy," she managed to mutter from a mouth gone dry.

"But surely you need to *eat*?" Javier stroked her with his words, and she shivered as her mind vividly flashed on the type of eating she'd really enjoy.

"I don't have time to play," she snapped, trying to break their mesmerizing spell.

"Then it shall be a business lunch," Javier announced, clapping his hands together and rubbing them.

"And exactly how do you figure you guys taking me to lunch is business?" she retorted. "I know what you both want to do with me, and while it might involve mergers, I deal in paper deals, not naked, fleshy ones."

"Dirty girl," Javier chided. "Did it eve occur to you that Ethan and I might have an interest in you that doesn't involve your luscious body?"

"No. I mean yes. Oh, for god's sake. Stop confusing me. You and I both know you're just saying you have work for me as a ploy to get me to go to lunch, because otherwise you know my answer would be no."

"It's not a scam," Ethan rumbled. "We need your help. With all of our freelance work and investments, not to mention our lacrosse and hockey monies, we need help getting organized. Don't forget, we only moved to Toronto from out west a month ago. We've been shopping around for an accountant and everyone says you're the best." Naomi tried not to preen at the praise. Ethan quirked a lip and shrugged. "We only play and deal with the best. So, yes, we would like to meet with you to discuss business because we'd like you to take over the accounting of our assets."

Naomi almost fell off her chair as Ethan spoke a veritable mouthful without stammering—or grunting. She wanted to hate that he kept destroying her stereotypical view of a jock, but instead she grudgingly liked him more and more. *The jerk.* "I don't come cheap," she replied when she should have just said no. But, she couldn't resist the lure of two new clients and the extra income. She wished she owned a mental muzzle for her inner wolf who spun in circles woofing while she chased her tail giddily.

Clapping his hands again, Javier grinned. "Price is no object. We'll pay you twice your rate. Trust me, given our extensive *assets*, you'll earn it." Javier winked as he said it and Naomi, for the third time in as many days, wanted to bang her head off something.

Caught in a losing battle—and barely raising a hand to fight the seemingly inevitable fate shoved her way—she could only faintly nod in agreement. In no time at all, she found herself ushered out of her office with Javier telling her secretary they'd return in a few hours.

Naomi wanted to protest their manhandling of her and her affairs; however, as if sensing her coming rebuttal, Ethan used a vicious weapon on her. Himself.

A giant paw lacking only fur and claws, gripped hers, lacing her digits in an intimate fashion that made her lose a step. Ethan rumbled, "While the goodnight kiss was great, I missed holding you last night, and waking up beside you."

The sincerity in his tone and expression almost melted her into a puddle. She wanted to rip him a new one. Wasn't she still after all mad over the free for all at her parent's house? Speaking of which, why did he look so unscathed? No one escaped a family get together without the bruises to prove it. She hadn't noticed the night before due to the encroaching gloom, but today, in the bright light of day, he appeared unhurt.

"How come you're not black and blue from dinner?" she demanded.

Javier answered and she pivoted to look at him. "We didn't grow up in nice neighborhoods. We know how to hold our own."

"You hurt my brothers and father?" she screeched. Never mind her family attacked them, blood came first.

"Of course not," Ethan retorted. "Much," he amended. "But any injuries they received were in self-defense and should already have healed."

"You forgot to mention the most important part. Not only did we not put them in a hospital," Javier interrupted. "We came to an agreement."

Wrinkling her brow, she stopped and gazed between them. "What kind of agreement?"

"After your mother explained your inherent dislike of violence, especially in family and home settings, we hammered out a deal. They won't interfere in your decision to take us as mates so long as you're the one to make the decision of how, when and where."

"How's never?" she snapped.

Javier continued on as if she hadn't spoken. "And from now on, if your brothers, or father, truly feel an urge to fight, we shall do so in a civilized fashion at the gym, in the practice ring, or in extreme situations, outdoors."

74

"Ha, good luck with that," she snorted. "I've lived in violent chaos all my life. I don't see my family changing just because you said so."

"They will," Ethan replied. "We won't let them upset you anymore."

Disbelief made her shake her head. "You're both delusional. There's no way you can enforce that rule. Don't forget, I grew up with them. Every male in my family has done their damned best to destroy everything I've ever owned, intentional or not. That's not going to change overnight. And to be quite honest, I highly doubt the pair of you will be any different. I bet you're both the type to drop the gloves and go at it instead of walking away or, gasp, talking first."

Ethan ducked his head, color rising in his cheeks. It didn't her give a triumphant feeling to know her assumption proved correct.

"We don't indulge in fights without provocation," Ethan muttered.

"And what's your idea of reasonable grounds? Forget it. I don't want to know. Shifters never seem to need a valid reason. You can't help it. Violence is in your blood."

"Your blood, too," Javier added.

She tossed her hair. "But I'm trying to fight my baser side. You two, on the other hand, aren't."

"Says who? I bet you we could control ourselves better than you." Javier taunted.

A snort escaped her. "Yeah right."

"Willing to put your assertion to the test? We bet you we can restrain ourselves from involving ourselves in any type of violence when around you."

"With the exception of sports," Ethan added.

Naomi's lips tightened. "I don't wager."

Javier's lips tilted and his eyes glinted with humor. "Come on? You seem so sure we can't rein in our baser impulses, what can it hurt?"

"Are you chicken?" Ethan added.

The glare she shot the behemoth's way was met with a shrug and a grin. "What's the prize?" she asked unable to stop her curiosity.

"You win and we will walk away, leaving you alone."

That didn't sound like much of a prize. "And if you both can control yourselves and not get involved in altercations when around me?"

"You let us make love to you."

"You mean mark me?"

"No." Javier shook his head. "Something so serious should not be decided on the outcome of a wager. We're talking about letting us worship your body as it deserves. Giving you extreme pleasure, which in turn will be the best reward we could hope for." His words painted a vivid picture of them kissing her, touching her, and...

Naomi's head nodded in agreement to the terms even as she knew it was such a bad idea. *Because dammit, now I want to lose, but how will that happen. These guys are born and bred brawlers. They'll never be able to keep their word.*

* * * * *

Javier could sense her inner conflict, in fact he prayed for it. Things had gone so well until the disastrous dinner of the night before. While he expected it of Ethan, Javier should have known better than to arouse Naomi in front of her brothers—until he'd marked her. However, the lure of her presence and worse, her interest, blinded him to their location with disastrous consequences.

Overprotective brothers had the right to defend their sister's honor, but Javier and Ethan grossly miscalculated on how a regular rumble, common in shifter households, would send Naomi running. It had only taken Meredith's quietly announced, "She left," for the fight to deflate. And that's when Javier discovered that despite her feisty nature, Naomi thought she wanted a life completely absent of violence. Probably not one hundred percent feasible given the hotheaded nature of shapeshifters—herself included—but he and Ethan came to an understanding with her family, her brothers especially. If they were to make this work, they needed to keep Naomi's needs in mind.

As for how they'd convinced the brothers, simple really. Ethan only had to say, "If you make her unhappy, once we mark her, we will take the offer to return and play for the Saskatoon, Coyote Wilds."

Amazing what moving her across a few provinces could do for negotiations, that and the fact Ethan had barely broken into a sweat when he'd held off four of the brothers by himself. Kodiak bears weren't a species to mess with.

Of course, Javier didn't relate his blackmail of her family to her when he made the bet. He treasured his balls too much for that.

Nor did it stop him, or Ethan, from attempting to seduce her with small touches and courtesies. In the restaurant, which he'd chosen because of the booths that would tuck her between them, he'd secretly thrilled— which disgusted him—at the innocuous squeeze of his legs against hers while they partook of their meal. As they discussed what duties they expected her to perform with their accounts, they'd briefly caress her hand. At times, Javier just sat back and watched her discourse with Ethan while he mentally detailed what other tasks he'd like her to accomplish for him—naked, maybe wearing some sexy glasses. Pleasant visuals that left him harder than a rock. *I can't wait until you accept us as your mates, sweetheart.*

Javier, to his utter surprise, had fallen for the vixen. He'd not realized just how badly she'd snared him until he realized other women no longer attracted him. He didn't even feel the slightest urge to flirt, not with Naomi's pretty receptionist, or the girl at the coffeehouse, and even though their current waitress kept leaning over in an attempt to show off her bosom, he couldn't help wishing Naomi would bend over instead—again, naked.

So much for thinking he'd live the life of a playboy spreading his love. There was only one woman he wanted to sink his cock into—bareback because, for the first time in his life, the concept of impregnating a woman filled him with satisfaction instead of knee jerking fear.

I am just as bad as Ethan with all these sappy thoughts running through my mind. He'd always scoffed at love in the past, but the more he saw and got to know Naomi, the more he wanted to discover. If that wasn't love then he obviously didn't have a clue. However, thinking he might have fallen for her didn't mean he'd announce it. She'd probably rip his nuts off and choke him with them for even suggesting it. *But hey, at least then she'd be touching me of her own volition.*

He hid his chuckles behind his napkin, but Naomi, watching more than he would have credited her with, narrowed her eyes suspiciously at him. Lunch ended, or so he assumed as the waitress swiped their plates, although, Javier couldn't recall what he'd eaten, if anything.

He ordered dessert for Naomi, despite her protests, then, almost sank under the table when it arrived. Ethan wore a glazed look that probably matched Javier's own as they stared, almost drooling, as she licked and sucked the caramel off her spoon. Her groaning enjoyment in her sundae almost destroyed his ability to think. Poor Ethan, he ended up closing his eyes, his jaw tight as he fought the lust she so easily—and maybe not so innocently—caused.

Javier thanked the cut of his jacket that covered his erection as they paid the bill and left. As they walked from the restaurant to his car, Ethan held her hand, while Javier stroked the middle of her back in the guise of leading her in the correct direction. From holding open the car door and seating her, to casually brushing her thigh with his fingers as he shifted, every innocent embrace burned and didn't go unanswered. The problem with heightening her senses and arousing her in bits and pieces that left her eyes glazed with burgeoning passion was the toll it took on their own bodies. Ethan looked fair ready to burst, and Javier, well, his hand was about to get a real workout if they couldn't get her to succumb to her desires soon.

The silence in the car hung thick enough to smack with his hard cock, the lust emanating from all three of them evident, yet unspoken. Javier knew without asking that Naomi wanted to return to her office instead of playing hooky and going back to her place or theirs for some afternoon frolicking. However, Javier couldn't just let her leave without attempting to see her again. Not finding a spot to park in front of her office building, he swung around the back into the alleyway, ignoring the no parking signs.

Stepping out of the car, immediately followed by Ethan who unfolded himself from the backseat, they both cornered her on the passenger side when she emerged through the door they held open. Shaking her head in bemusement, she took a few steps forward and Ethan slammed the door shut behind her, startling her.

"I should get back to work," she said, her shiver as Ethan brushed up against her back not going unnoticed.

"First, tell me we can take you to dinner tonight?" Javier swayed toward her, unable to resist her allure, his hand brushing a stray hair from her cheek.

Her pulse sped up and her eyes dilated. She unconsciously leaned back into Ethan, which only heightened her trembling. "I-I can't," she whispered, licking her lips.

Javier almost groaned. He wanted to suck on her tongue so bad. "Why not?"

"I, um, kind of have a date."

Jealousy, a heretofore unknown feeling, hit him and made his inner cat's hackles rise and Javier's brows shoot up to the sky. "Excuse me?" I don't think so." Irrational, commanding words he just couldn't prevent himself from uttering.

Ethan growled, the possessive sound of his beast showing his intent dislike of her plans.

Naomi blinked and pushed away from them, her cool exterior sliding back into place and concealing the temptress hidden in her curvy body. A smirk made her lips tilt. "Oh, I do think so. I have a date with a very accomplished lawyer, a human one, who graduated fourth in his class. He's also quite handsome, not to mention financially established." Javier's jaw tightened, while Ethan bared his teeth in a snarl. "Go ahead," she taunted. "Get mad and break something. You know you want to. Not even a day and already about to lose your bet."

Eyes narrowed at her goading, Javier didn't give in to the temptation to do what she said. He'd break something later out of her sight. "You know he can't give you what you want. What you *need.*"

"You're meant for us," Ethan grumbled.

"Actually, Phil has a lot to offer, starting with the fact he belongs to the chess club instead of the fight one. Now, if you'll excuse me. I need to finish up my work so I can get ready for my hot date." She winked at them and blew them a kiss. "Later."

And with that, the minx sashayed off, her hips swinging.

Teeth gnashing, Javier fought to not run after her and scoop her up caveman style. *Infuriating, delicious vixen.* Rejection sucked.

"I don't like this," rumbled Ethan.

"Me neither. But don't worry. I have a plan." A wickedly diabolical one. *Sweetheart, you shouldn't have thrown down the gauntlet like that because now, I'm going to play dirty. And oh, are you going to like it.*

81

Chapter Eight

Bored. So bloody bored. Naomi tried to listen to Phil as he droned on and on about his successful practice. She tried to focus on his face, but his weak chin, which she'd never really noticed before, and pasty white skin made her wish for tanned and muscled…

Nope. I don't miss or want those two testosterone laden idiots. She tried to imagine kissing Phil, letting him touch her with his soft hands and couldn't stop a shudder. *Okay, so he's not the man for me.* It didn't mean Sexy and Sexier were. *But wanting to screw their brains out and chaining myself to them for life are two totally opposite things.* And if she didn't fear the former would lead to the latter, she would have probably just scratched her carnal itch. She still might if she could only assure herself they wouldn't try and trick her in a moment of weakness.

A prickling sensation tickled the back of her neck and she turned to see what had caught her attention. Her jaw dropped as Javier and Ethan strode into the restaurant with blonde bimbos clinging to their arms. Naomi gritted her teeth and her nails—which elongated into partial claws—poked bloody crescents into her palms as she furiously told herself she wasn't jealous. *Not at all. Why do I care? It's not like we're an item even if they keep telling me they want me. Two-timing jerks.*

Pivoting back, she refused to look at them any further and concentrated on Phil. Stupid, boring Phil. His lips moved, but she didn't have the slightest clue, or interest, in what he said. Instead of paying attention to her date, she found herself trying to tune in to what occurred behind her. Low murmurs and shrill, bubbly laughter made her gnash her teeth and her inner wolf, howled in irritation.

"Excuse me. I need to go to the ladies room." Naomi stood abruptly, leaving Phil midsentence. Quick strides brought her out of the main dining area and into the washroom where she braced her hands on the sink and peered in the mirror.

Anger glittered in her eyes making them bright and feral. Her cheeks held red spots of color while her lips were pulled tight against her teeth. She looked completely and utterly pissed. *Dammit.* How long was she going to lie to and deny herself? *I want those two sexy idiots, not boring, safe Phil.*

The admission didn't please her.

Time to go home. Wanting them didn't mean she'd degrade herself by going to them begging or acting the jealous shrew.

Exiting the bathroom, she ran into a solid wall. A familiar scent tickled her nose as big hands braced her around the waist, steadying her.

"Ethan, what are you doing here?" She looked up at him, questioning and breathless at his closeness.

A tug was all it took for him to draw her nearer, and she didn't resist. Eyes of soft brown peered down at her. "You're mad," he stated sounding pleased.

"When aren't I?" she retorted.

"I like it even if drives me wild," he admitted. "I can't stop thinking of you."

Self-preservation made her tone sharp. "Gee, you could have fooled me. Seems to me you're recovering quite well with that blonde, overdone slut."

A ghost of a smile lifted the corners of his lips and satisfaction glinted in his eyes. "You're jealous."

"Am not," she retorted, lying unashamedly.

"Liar," he chided. "And those blondes weren't for Javier and me."

When her brow creased in puzzlement, he urged her to follow him, his solid arm an anchor around her upper body. Arriving back into the restaurant proper, they ran into Javier who looked entirely too smug.

A grin lit his face. "Naomi, you look absolutely delicious."

"Shouldn't you be saying that to your date?" Her reply came out tart and went well with her arched brow.

"Why Ethan, is it me or is that jealousy I hear?"

A chuckle made the behemoth's body shake beside her and she jabbed her elbow back sharply turning it into a wheeze.

Naomi pursed her lips and narrowed her eyes. "I don't know what game you two are playing, but count me out. I need to get back to my date."

"Yeah, about that…"Javier stepped aside and Naomi gaped as Phil's flushed face came into view. The reason? The two scantily dressed bimbos draped over him. The anger she'd experienced when those same girls were hanging off Ethan and Javier didn't emerge. Actually, a vague relief suffused her. Amusement colored Javier's tone when he spoke. "We thought we'd test your friend by throwing temptation his way. I'm afraid he's failed. We on the other hand, had no problem resisting them."

"You did that on purpose," she accused.

"Yes, we did." Javier looked completely unashamed of his naughty trick. But, he wasn't the only one who could play dirty.

"Maybe not the best decision giving up two sure things. I guess I'm not the only one going home to my five fingers tonight," she taunted before sashaying off. Temptation to see their faces almost made her turn around to see their reaction, but she didn't want to ruin her exit. Besides, she feared begging them to use their five fingers—actually make that twenty between the two of them—to cure what ailed her.

* * * * *

Ethan shook mostly in lust, but also shock. "Did she just say what I think she did?"

Javier's lips quirked into a grin as he nodded his head. "She is something isn't she? Come on. I know where she's parked. It wouldn't do for her to end her date without a kiss."

Ethan followed his friend as they weaved through the tables following the delectable ass of their woman. She wore a slim fitting, ruby colored sheath that clung to her curves and made Ethan gnash his teeth and strive for control as he couldn't help notice the appreciative glances thrown her way.

When he'd walked in and seen her sitting with that puny human, he'd almost lost his cool. His bear had roared in his mind, ready to charge over and tear the daring human into itty bitty pieces. However, the icy glare Naomi had tossed their way at the sight of their pretend dates did much to restore his calm and kept him following Javier's plan. A brilliant plan actually that didn't require any violence—on their part at least—thus allowing them to keep their word.

He and Javier caught up to Naomi just outside the restaurant. Ethan clasped her hand before she could protest and linked his fingers through hers. Javier aped him on the other side and she sighed aloud.

"You guys just don't give up, do you?"

"You're mine. Ours." Ethan saw no reason to couch his feelings.

Javier chuckled. "As Ethan so eloquently put it, since we've met you, you've never been far from our minds. We want you, in our bed and in our lives."

"You want to mark me and make me your little shifter slave."

"We want to mark you to show the world you belong to us. If anyone's a slave, it's us for wanting to give you the moon."

They reached her car and she pulled from their grasp. Turning to face them, she leaned back against her vehicle.

"You haven't yet proven yourselves to me. For all I know, you're just enjoying the thrill of the chase."

Javier's brows shot up as he looked at Ethan. "She says we didn't prove anything? I'd say the fact we gave your date two women to compensate him for losing you instead of ripping his head off for looking at you was a pretty good example of our control."

Naomi's lips twitched and when she smiled, Ethan almost fell to his knees in worship. Stunning. Absolutely stunning, and if he wasn't mistaken also thawing toward them.

"Don't think you've won the wager yet," she actually teased. "That won't be decided until the next family get-together."

"But don't we deserve a small prize at least," Javier murmured moving closer to her. His hands palmed her waist and drew her forward. As if a signal, Ethan moved in behind her, brushing his big body up against her back as Javier cuddled her front. Her head tilted back, exposing her neck and her lashes swept down as Javier caught her lips in a sensual kiss. Ethan felt a moment's regret his friend got to taste her, but only for a moment before his own mouth latched onto the smooth skin of her neck. Sucking at her tender skin and feeling the rapid beat of her pulse against his tongue excited him almost as much.

Placing his hands on her hips to hold her steady, Ethan gyrated his erection against her plush backside, cursing the clothes that separated their skin. Her low moan of response made him shudder and the perfume of her arousal almost made him bite her, his beast clamoring to mark this woman and then take her like her body so obviously craved.

But, I am a man, not an animal. I won't force her. I want her to choose me.

Ethan sensed more than saw Javier's hands moving up to cup her heavy breasts, but he could imagine Javier's thumbs brushing across her peaks, tightening them into buds ready for sucking. A need to touch her—intimately—drove him to slide his right hand, the one hidden from public view by the car, down to the short hem of her skirt. He dragged the silken material up, his knuckles brushing the smooth skin of her thighs.

Her soft cry of surprise was caught by Javier's mouth, but Ethan felt the slight tremble in her limbs as he let his hand rove around to the front of her body. Her thighs were clamped together so he pressed the heel of his hand against her pubes, still covered by the thin silk of her panties.

Slowly, he rotated his hand against her, the scorching heat making him pant in need. When she eased her thighs apart, he almost melted. Lightly, he let his fingers run along her cleft, the damp fabric showing her excitement better than words.

He slid his finger under the elastic and tickled it over the lips of her sex. Her knees buckled, but Javier grabbed her and held her steady, capturing her mewling cries with his mouth as Ethan continued to explore her pussy. He parted her lips and penetrated her with one digit, then two. The moist walls of her channel clamped onto him. Swallowing hard at her eagerness, he worked his fingers in and out while allowing his thumb to rub against her clit. He buried his face in the curve of her neck, the torture of pleasing her almost too much to bear.

Her sudden climax forced the silken walls of her sex to convulse and squeeze around his digits. *Damn, but I wish it was my cock in there instead.* Ethan's free arm clung to her, pushing her tight against him as he ground himself against her ass while she rode his fingers hard.

It took a shouted, "Get a room," to bring him back to reality. Unfortunately, it also broke the spell of sensuality they'd woven around Naomi.

She pulled away from them and his fingers slipped out of her with reluctance. Her eyes stared at them wildly. "Oh, no. That did not just happen."

"It's all right—"

She cut Javier off. "No, it's not. I don't do things like this. Especially not in public."

"No one saw anything," Ethan replied.

Her glare made him flinch. "Proper humans, like I want to be, don't have orgasms in a parking lot with two men. Oooh." Her inarticulate cry of frustration wounded him along with the confusion in her eyes.

Ethan wanted to speak, but Javier shook his head. It killed him to watch Naomi climb into her car with shaking hands, then peal out of the parking lot. They ended up not far behind her in Javier's Lexus.

"Why did you stop me?" Ethan growled watching Naomi's erratic flight.

Javier weaved through the traffic after her. "She's not ready."

"She felt plenty ready to me," Ethan bit out, the scent of her on his hand driving him wild.

"We provided relief for her physical need. She is not ready, though, to give us her heart and to give up her foolish belief she can be happy living as a human. But fear not, my friend, she's close to changing her mind."

"Yeah, well, I hope she figures it out a little more quickly because I don't know how much more of this I can take."

"Aah, but think of the pleasure when she finally comes to us."

Ethan shot him a dark look. "And if it takes a year or more."

"Then I'd better not drop any soap while in the shower, I guess."

Their laughter rocked the car as they ensured Naomi made it home safe. Then they roared in mirth again as she flipped them the middle finger before stomping up her porch steps and slamming into the house.

She is so bloody perfect.

Javier, now that he'd assured himself Naomi had made it home safely, pulled away from the curb. Ethan's phone rang and he pulled it out, groaning at the number. "Not again."

"Who is it?" Javier asked as he drove them back to their condo.

"Maurice again." Their old coach from the Coyote Wilds. Since their decision to transfer for better money and a change of scenery, he hadn't stopped trying to entice them back.

"Might as well tell him. You and I both know we won't move her away from her family."

"He's not going to be happy. Not when we've had him jumping through hoops catering to our demands to come back." Not that they had any intention. Maurice had also played a part in their leaving with his heavy-handed tactics.

"Too bad," Javier replied.

Clicking the answer button, Ethan put the phone to his ear.

"Ethan, I've been trying to get a hold of you." Maurice's deep voice didn't sound too happy, not that Ethan gave a damn. Their previous team owner and coach seemed to have a permanent burr up his ass. It was part of the reason they'd ditched his team to transfer to the Ottawa Loup Garou's.

"Hey Maurice. Listen, sorry we didn't get back to you sooner. We've got some good and bad news. Good news, we've met our mate. Bad news is we're not coming back."

"Both of you?"

"Well, it's actually the same girl. Anyway, we're still kind of courting her because she's not into the whole mate claiming thing, but even once we do, we won't be coming back. Her family lives here and she's real close to them."

"You've not even marked her yet and you're turning me down? What if things don't turn out? Do you really want to stay in the same town? Shifter circles are small ones."

Ethan shook his head. Maurice knew as well as they did, once the mating fever hit, it was only a matter of time. "Yeah, well, Javier says it won't be long. We've got a plan."

"I see." Maurice got quiet and Ethan feared he'd hung up—or died of a stroke finally cluing in that his star players were never coming back. "Well, I guess the only thing to do is wish you guys good luck. I look forward to us kicking your ass in our next match. And remember, if you guys change your mind and want to relocate, I'll meet all your terms."

"Gee, thanks, Maurice. If it's any consolation, up until we met her, we really were leaning toward coming back." Ethan rolled his eyes as he lied. "But you know how it is."

"Yeah, I do. Bye."

Maurice hung up and Ethan looked over at Javier. "I guess this means we'd better stock up on winter clothing. I hear the winters in Ottawa are a bitch."

"Ah, but we'll have one very hot wolf to keep us warm, though, won't we."

Ethan grinned in reply and made a mental note to have a fireplace installed in whatever home they ended up buying for Naomi because he could already picture her naked on the floor in front it as they idled the snowy winter hours away—on a synthetic fur rug, of course, anything else would just be plain wrong or possibly related to him.

Chapter Nine

Grumpy didn't come close to describing Naomi's state of mind the next day. Hornier than hell. Tired. Annoyed. Those came close and yet none of those terms completely explained the turmoil boiling inside her.

The previous evening, still shaking from her unexpected parking lot climax, she'd barely made it home. Her body—and wolf—howled at her to go back and take what they offered.

However, that stank too much of submission. *And I hate not being in control.*

Slamming into her house after flipping the causes of her displeasure off, she'd actually waited with almost bated breath for them to come pounding on her door. Begging her to kiss them goodnight. To resume what they'd started. She'd even partially fantasized about them, overcome with lust, pushing their way into her home, and taking her, right up against the wall.

Instead, they'd left. The jerks. And she'd gone upstairs to a big, lonely bed with an aching pussy that still quivered faintly in remembrance at Ethan's touch. Actually, she still ached today, sitting in her office chair, her cotton panties damp and chafing.

No fair. Why couldn't I have felt like this for Phil or some other normal guy who won't make my life a chaotic hell?

She loved the calm orderliness of her home and life. She still loved her family, but she much preferred weekly visits to the day-to-day violence rampant in a household with six oversized males. If she let Javier and Ethan into her life, what would she condemn herself to? Would her home require a bucket of plaster and paint on hand for mishaps? How would her delicate collection of butterflies survive? *But without them, how will I stay sane?*

Another pencil snapped between her fingers and, with a sigh, she tossed it in her garbage pail to join the other half dozen she'd destroyed already today with her tenseness. Checking her email, she discovered the lawyer for the uncle on that possible fraud situation had replied to her missive the previous evening around six p.m.

Hey Naomi,

I spoke to the uncle and he got pretty in my face over the implication he might be playing around with the children's money. He's claiming he just forgot to send in some receipts for stuff the kids needed. But I don't know, he seemed pretty pissed, and I kind of got the impression he wasn't on the up and up. As per your recommendation, I've frozen the accounts until we can dig a little deeper and he coughs up those supposed receipts.

Good eye for spotting it. Let me know if you find anything concrete on your end, and I'll do the same from my side.

George

She skimmed through the rest of her emails, most of it minor stuff that could wait. At the bottom of the list, she noticed a second email sent by George that morning at the ungodly hour of five a.m.

Ignore the previous message. Audit not needed. We'll talk later.

Short and to the point, it raised every single hackle she owned. She grabbed her phone and dialed his office number, but his direct line went straight to voicemail. She left a message for him to call her and made a note to try again later.

Lunchtime arrived and Naomi caught herself drumming her fingers on her desktop, watching the door. It remained closed. Josie had taken the day off to volunteer for her daughter's class trip. The minutes ticked by and Naomi frowned. Chewing on a granola bar she found in her drawer, she slammed things around on her desk, irritated and it certainly wasn't because of disappointment they hadn't shown. *I am such a liar.*

Her phone rang and she dove on it. "Hello, Bitten By Numbers Accounting, how may I help you?"

"Hey, baby girl," her mother said. "Why are you at work instead of lying in bed?"

Naomi leaned back in her chair. "I know I am going to regret asking this, but why would I be in bed?"

"Well, I could barely walk after your father claimed me; more times than I could count, the horny devil. I figured since you managed to snag two strapping men, you'd probably need more time to recover."

"Oh, eew! Mom!" She didn't know what was worse—the mental image of her parents actually doing it, which she'd walked in on once—talk about scarring—or the fact her mother was talking about her getting fucked so hard she couldn't walk. On a disturbing scale of one to ten, they both ranked in the twenties.

"Oh, don't play innocent with me. It's not like you're a virgin. Heck, the whole neighborhood knew when you lost it. You made such a fuss about it."

Poor Tommy, in his enthusiasm to breach her after she said yes, he'd hurt her more than he intended. His screams as he ran down the street, her hot on his ass pelting rocks at his bare backside had raised a few eyebrows. His family ended up moving, they had to when her brothers wouldn't stop stalking Tommy and detailing ways they were going to remove the cock that tainted their sister. Since her disastrous first time, Naomi had enjoyed a few sexual encounters. *Although none of them came close making me feel the way I do with my two bloody jocks.* The sensations they could evoke with the simplest of looks and touches made her wonder if the main event could truly live up to expectation.

"Hello? Earth to Naomi? Are you still there?"

Her mother's voice acted like a cold shower on the lusty train of her thoughts. "I'm here. Did you just call me to embarrass me or did you have another purpose in mind?"

"I take it you're still being stubborn. You're a Lycan, Naomi. Lycans meet their mates, fuck and mark each other."

"And then live happily ever after blah, blah, blah. Yes, I know. And wow, talk about eloquent. Now I really want to run out and hitch myself. Not!"

"Don't take that tone with me. I don't know why you're so reticent about it. I'd have thought your dad and I would be a prime example of opposites working out."

True, after thirty five years, her parents still managed to make everyone sick with how much they cared for each other. It would have probably even been cute with anyone else's parents. "But what about the chaos, mom? I can't do it. I won't. Don't you ever get tired of it?"

Her mother let out a long sigh. "Oh, Naomi. Not all households are like ours. I'll admit, your brothers and father are a rough bunch, but they're big boys. They get excited."

"Excited? They're like bulls in china shops, who I might add, should have moved out by now."

"They will when they meet their mates. Besides, you and I both know boys take longer to mature."

Naomi snorted. "What's dad's excuse then?"

"I like him rough and raw around the edges. Not all of us want some effeminate pansy, you know."

A choking sound escaped her. "Mom, I never said I wanted a pansy."

"Says you. If you ask me, you don't know what you want, or worse, you do, but you're scared to admit it. Javier and Ethan are good looking, polite, and smart. Three items on your list."

"They're also jocks in a pair of violent sports."

"So they have a place to let off some steam. Cut them some slack. You can fight it, baby girl, but in the end, you'll just fall harder."

"Says you."

"Says someone who's seen it before. What? Did you think you're the first one to fight fate? Guess what darling, it never works. Add to that the low divorce rate in mated couples and I don't see the big deal."

"The deal is I like my life and I like my things and I'm not going to let anybody, not even my wolf, tell me what I have to do."

Her mother cackled. "Oh. You always were my favorite."

"You say to that to all of us, mom."

"And I mean it. See you at dinner on Sunday?"

"Of course. Love you."

They said goodbye and hung up, but her mother's accusations and reminders sat heavily on her mind. *Am I making mountains out of molehills?* Maybe. However, it wasn't in her nature to give into anything easily, not even love.

Banging her head on her desk a few times, she tried to reassure herself that her Freudian slip of the word love was really meant to be lust. Nevertheless, once spoken, even if only in her mind, it hovered there taunting her. She buried herself in her work in an attempt to forget it.

The rest of the afternoon proved a write-off because she just couldn't stay focused. How stupid of her to assume they would make lunch with her a daily habit, or at least pop by and say hello. It was even dumber of her to experience disappointment when they didn't. *I don't want them in my life, so why am I on pins and needles wondering when I'll see them again?* Horniness or not, she'd never felt like this for anyone else, and this out of control sensation pissed her off.

Much too distracted to work, she decided to call it a day. She grabbed her bag and locked up her office on the sixth floor. She took the elevator down to the basement parking garage where she paid a hefty premium to reserve a spot for her baby.

Heels clicking loudly on the pavement, she strutted to her car, eager to get out of here and into the sunshine. There she could open up the top, slam the pedal to the metal and let the wind rush through her hair. Addicted to speed, her brothers joked she should have chosen a career as an Indy car driver.

The section she'd parked in loomed ahead of her, darkly shadowed as the fluorescent lighting in the area appeared broken. She made a note to call maintenance in the morning if they didn't repair it overnight. While she didn't fear for her safety, the human women in the building needed all the security they could get.

Even with the gloom, though, she noticed the wrong looking aspect of her car. Her confident steps stuttered to a halt.

"Oh, no. No. No!" Her baby, her precious car she'd scrimped and gone without for, that she'd lovingly hand-washed for years and maintained like the pickiest of mother's, was ruined. Killed. Demolished in a heinous crime of violence.

Naomi let out a wail and rushed to the crumpled hood, her shaking hands running in disbelief over the dents and scratches. The windshield gaped toothily at her with its pointed glass shards. The honeycombed chunks, smashed free, adorned the torn leather seats. And the convertible top? Slashed to tatters.

Clenching her fists to her sides, she strove for calm—and failed miserably. *How could someone do this?* Theft she could understand, but to destroy an innocent car so completely?

A fragment of white on her steering column caught her attention and she reached in to grab it, the block letters mocking her with their anonymity.

Back off. They don't need you messing up their life. Consider this a warning.

Naomi's lips peeled back from her teeth and she growled, her bitch perilously close to the surface, eager to hunt the malefactor down. She flipped the sheet over and peered for identifying marks, but in the dark, even with her enhanced eyesight, she couldn't make out any fine details, if any, the threatening note contained. It also lacked a signature.

Coward. Why couldn't you leave me your name so I'd know who to kill?

But she had a good idea—one certain uncle who'd gotten caught with his hand in the money jar.

A feral grin stretched across her face and her teeth sharpened into points as her wolf pushed at the surface of her psyche. *Oh, you little bastard. You messed with the wrong bitch. Before, I might have given you an inch, now I'm going to make your life a living monetary hell.*

First though, she'd arrange a tow for her car and request an estimate on repairs, probably an astronomical sum considering the work needed to bring her baby back to life. Of course, the screaming she'd do when she got that bill would pale in comparison to that of her family

98

when they heard of the threat. Naomi sighed as she dialed her parent's house for a ride.

I guess there's no way of avoiding a little chaos and violence this time. Actually, this is one occasion where it's completely justified.

* * * * *

Javier cursed as he hung up his phone. "No fucking way."

Ethan, riding their home exercise bike, glanced over at him. "Are you swearing? Must be bad. What's up?"

"Somebody trashed Naomi's car at work."

Quicker than a blink, Ethan's bear took over and a roar echoed from his mouth as his teeth elongated, his body reshaped and fur sprouted. In seconds, a pissed Kodiak, wearing only shreds of clothing, lumbered toward the apartment door and Javier sprinted to throw himself in front of Ethan.

"Stop! You can't go out there like that. Are you out of your fucking mind?"

A growl was the reply as Ethan butted Javier with his big shaggy head, tossing him aside. Javier landed on his hands and flipped to a standing position. "If you get shot or picked up by animal control, you won't be able to protect her, dumbass."

Javier's cool logic stopped Ethan from clawing the door off. It didn't save it, though. The inch deep gouges would probably never sand out, but at least it remained on its hinges. A heavy thump sounded as the bear sat, somehow managing to appear disgruntled. Javier let out a breath.

He couldn't blame his friend for his reaction. Knowing that someone had destroyed something of Naomi's, something she loved, made his jaguar yowl and his claws come out. But, he knew violence and rushing off without thinking wouldn't solve anything. *Calm and methodical stalking is always the better recourse.*

"Listen. You're obviously going to be stuck here for a little bit while your bear calms down and you regain enough energy for a shift. We both don't need to go get her. According to her dad, she's fine, but extremely pissed. She's waiting for a ride in the front lobby with the building security guard."

Ethan chuffed, sounding amused even in animal form.

Javier gave him a wry grin. "I know. She's probably tougher than a half dozen human security guards, but at least she's in a public place with cameras. She's obviously pretty upset. We both heard how much she loves that car from her mom."

Ethan shook his head and made some grumbling noises.

"If you're saying we should just buy her a new one, then the answer is no. She wouldn't accept it; although, we can talk to the mechanic and toss some money his way to make sure his quote isn't too much for her. Now, as I was saying, we're not both needed to grab her, and given your current indisposition, why don't I go fetch her? You can meet us back at her place. Maybe get some food and something to cheer her up on the way? And bring the overnight bags."

A nod of his shaggy head and Javier's grin faded. "Don't worry, Ethan. Once we've made arrangements for her safety, we will find out who did this. They will not get away with it." The fangs Ethan flashed him made

Javier smile back just as viciously. "And they will regret it."

Javier thanked his lucky stars he'd left Ethan at home when he reached Naomi's work because she'd not only left the main lobby, she'd gone back down to the parking lot and her car. Javier located her crouched with her face almost pressed to the ground, inhaling.

"What the hell are you doing?" he spat, his words tight and controlled as he tried to keep his cat caged, an almost impossible feat when he saw the damage done to her car. *What if she'd come upon them while they wreaked havoc?* This type of destruction went beyond vandalism and reeked of intentional threat.

She ignored him—no surprise—and continued to sniff the pavement.

"Naomi," he growled through gritted teeth, his formidable patience wearing thin.

Sighing, she stopped her sleuthing and straightened. Turning, she placed her hands on her hips, her expression ripe with annoyance. "What are you doing here? I called my dad to come get me, not you."

"Who then called me, like you should have!" Javier met her, glare for glare.

Her lips pursed. "One, you don't own me, so why the hell would I call you? And two, while you were busy sticking your tongue down my throat, groping my tits and sticking your hands up my skirt, neither of you ever bothered to give me your number. Which, I might add, is not a request for them, and brings me back to my first point of you don't own me. Now go away while I deal with this. I'll just grab a cab after I see my car to the garage."

"You are out of your fucking mind if you think I'm leaving, sweetheart. I'll stay with you until we get

101

your car settled. But make no mistake, I will be taking you home."

Narrowed eyes and tight lips warned him that Naomi was about to explode. "I am not a little human weakling in need of protection. I can handle myself."

"I never said you couldn't. However, I, on the other hand, am just a Neanderthal male with a weak heart who needs to assure myself of your safety so I can sleep better tonight."

Her full lips quirked in amusement before she caught herself. "You are so pigheaded. Don't you get it yet that I'm not interested? Does the word no mean nothing to you? Do us both a favor and leave."

Javier crossed his arms over his chest and leaned against a concrete pillar. A ghost of a smile hovered on his lips. "Make me."

Annoyance glinted in her gaze—and if he wasn't mistaken, smoldering interest and her jaw tightened. "Don't tempt me."

Javier goaded her, needing distraction from the mess behind her, from the obvious violence directed at his mate. "Oh, I forgot. You're Miss Peace and Serenity. A little girl who can't hold her own against a real male, which is why you play with puny humans." Javier held himself ready for the fireworks.

A husky chuckle burst from her instead of rage. Smiling at him, a sensual curve bowing her lips, Naomi sashayed toward him, the sway of her hips hypnotic. A part of him warned to stay on guard, to not trust her seemingly benign appearance as she approached.

"Are you trying to make me angry? Because it's working," she said softly, stepping right up to him, so close he could feel the heat from her body.

Then he felt cold, hard concrete as she swept his feet out from under him, sending him down in a single, fluid movement. Before he could recover, or yell his shock, she straddled him. Her skirt rode up around her waist while her bare thighs gripped his head. Provocative as the pose proved, the true distraction resided further south where a cruel grasp squeezed his balls most painfully.

Flashing eyes, belonging to one triumphant and glorious woman, met his. "I really hate the fact that you all drive me to cave into my baser side. I abhor violence. How many times do I have to say it? I am a delicate. Freakn'. Flower!" She punctuated her claim with a twist of his nuts that made his breath whoosh out.

"I get it. I won't piss you off again," Javier gasped, partially in pain, partially in titillation because this close to her cleft, he could smell her. And, oh, did he want a taste. On second thought, why not?

He flicked his tongue out—the long, raspy tongue of a feline—and swiped it across her inner thigh.

"Oh." Her soft exclamation of surprise also came with her thighs tightening reflexively. *Oh, to feel that squeeze around my waist as I plow her.* Javier licked again and the grip on his sac eased, but she didn't remove her hand. It rested on his groin which expanded, straining at the confines of his pants.

Javier tilted his head as best he could towards her sex, her musk surrounding him and driving him wild. He longed to taste her. To plunge his tongue into her sex and stroke her with it until she came screaming his name. He could smell how she wanted it too. Even better, he could also see it in the way her eyes—heavy lidded and smoky—gazed down at him with her lips parted on a soft sigh.

The damned tow truck driver, though, had a lousy sense of timing. At the first rumble of the diesel engine, she bounced up and smoothed down her skirt, hiding the evidence of her arousal, but unable to do anything about her flushed cheeks and bright eyes, a good look for his feisty she-wolf.

Javier stood up more slowly, his aching nuts alternating with his throbbing, hard cock. *Hot damn, she's like a volcano ready to explode.* He couldn't wait to feel the burn.

Mental note to self: *Next time make sure we're both naked before I piss her off.* It didn't take a genius to realize, despite her claims she desired a chaos and violence free life, her hot temper and even more boiling blood would always ensure fabulous fireworks. *I guess Ethan and I will find out if makeup sex is all it's cracked-up to be.* It almost made him want to pull the wolf's tail right that instant to find out.

Chapter Ten

While she would never admit out loud, Naomi actually found herself glad of Javier's support. The process of getting her broken car on the flatbed tow truck proved hard to watch as bits and pieces fell off, clanging to the floor, or in the case of the broken glass, in a tinkling shower. Naomi alternated between rage and melancholy, her emotions in such a fluctuating state, she didn't object when he draped an arm around her shoulders and kept her hugged tight to his body.

Even more surprising was Javier's calmness. If her dad or brothers had shown up and seen the mess the thug made of her car, a copious amount of yelling and punching of things would have occurred. With Javier, while she could see ire in the flashing of his dark eyes and the rigidity of his jaw, those were the only outward signs. She appreciated it, but a teensy tiny part of her kind of wanted him to rant and rave, to show vocally and physically how much he cared.

I'm such an indecisive ninny.

It took a while before they were able to leave the garage. The mechanic's shaking head as he surveyed the damage not exactly an encouraging sign.

"I don't know, Naomi," said the grizzled wolf—her dad's brother and favored uncle—who worked as head mechanic. "It might be better to simply buy a new car and write this one off."

Tears flooded her eyes and she wandered away from Javier and her uncle Ken, the only male she trusted with her baby. She ignored their murmurs as she stroked the crumpled hood. *Not fair. I worked my ass off to get her.* Somehow, it seemed wrong to just toss her car out because someone had a grudge against her. *But, how will I ever manage to pay to for the repairs?*

Shoulders slumped, she didn't protest when Javier's hand landed on the middle of her back, guiding her away from the wreck. She let him seat her in his car for the ride home, too depressed to protest.

The first few minutes of the drive, she stayed silent, peering out the window at the whizzing streetlights. Cocooned in the cabin of his car, his scent surrounded her, reminding her she wasn't alone. A male had finally come to her aid and proven beneficial. What a novelty not having to babysit, apologize for or rein in someone who under the guise of help, just made things worse, say, like her brothers. It deserved an acknowledgement.

"Thanks for coming to get me," she muttered.

"Anytime, sweetheart. I want you to know, you will always be able to count on Ethan and I. No matter what."

Her lips twisted into a wry grin. "You just don't give up, do you?"

Turning his head sideways, Javier winked before he flashed her a hundred watt grin. "You aren't the only stubborn one around here. You'll soon see we're not like other shifters. For one, we're much better looking."

A snort escaped her. "And conceited, too."

"I prefer to use the term honest."

"So you say. I guess only time will tell." She fell silent again, and in the quiet, to her embarrassment, her stomach rumbled.

Javier chuckled. "I think someone's hungry. Good thing Ethan's waiting for us at your house. I called ahead and made sure he ordered in some food."

His words snapped her discomfiture. "You did what? Wait a second, how the hell did he get in?" She slapped her forehead. "Wait, let me guess. My mother gave you her spare key?" Meddlesome parent. Naomi really needed to have another talk with her mother about letting her make her own choices. Not that she expected her to listen. *I'm sure if mom owned a shotgun she would have used it by now to force a wedding.*

"She's just got your best interests at heart," Javier said softly.

"She's encouraging me to sleep with two guys because our beasts, or fate, or whatever power directs us, says we should."

"Would it be so bad?"

"You and Ethan don't stand to lose anything. Me, I lose my freedom and quiet existence." And she'd gain incredible pleasure. However, there was more to life than lust. While she knew they'd be able to provide for her, and they weren't as dumb as she'd initially thought, she still didn't know much about their character. How they were with kids. How they dealt with adversity. If they planned on making love to her together or one at a time.

Her eyes widened at the last thought. Exactly how would a dual mating work? Did they plan on swapping her back and forth, maybe designating days to have sex with her? Or would they pleasure her together—twice the cock, tongue and fingers.

Somehow she got the impression they did everything as a pair. *Oh my.*

"Mating is not a prison. Think of it as expanding your horizons." He stopped speaking and sniffed the air. She could almost see his body tense up as he growled low, "What's got you blushing and smelling delicious?"

The burn in Naomi's cheeks got hotter as he perceptively caught the external evidence of her inner thoughts. "N-nothing," she stuttered. No way would she tell him. Besides, she wasn't supposed to be interested. *Liar,* her subconscious chided.

"Better tuck your naughty thoughts aside for later. It looks like we've got company."

Naomi peered ahead through the windshield and groaned as she saw the cars parked outside her place. *My family to the rescue—more like destructive warpath.* She cringed, wondering at the damage probably already awaiting her inside.

As if reading her mind, Javier said, "Don't worry. Ethan will have made them behave."

"That's usually what starts it, though," she grumbled. Her mother would tell her brothers to stop. Then, one would point to another and say he was to blame. And thus chaos would erupt and a trip to the local furniture store would ensure in the aftermath.

Javier's fingers laced through hers as they headed up the walkway to her home. She didn't pull away, glad of his comfort. She would probably need it when she saw the interior of her home, and god help her family if they'd broken her butterflies!

They walked in to a scene of eerie silence, and to her relief, not a sign of destruction anywhere. Her brothers and father sat on the pair of couches, their bodies stiff. They turned their heads almost as one to glare at her, but they didn't say a word.

"Gee, make me feel welcome in my home," she snapped.

"They're just worried about you, sweetheart," Javier cajoled, his arm squeezing her.

Ethan came out of the kitchen, barefoot and wearing low-slung jeans and a t-shirt that delineated his upper body. He smiled at her and Naomi couldn't help the fluttery happy feeling at seeing him again. His brown eyes softened as if he knew. "Just in time. The Chinese food just arrived."

"Don't you think we have more pressing things to do than eat?" Stu muttered, his brows drawn so close together they almost formed a seamless line.

"Yeah, like hunting down some asshole and kicking his ass," Kendrick added along with the smacking sound of his fist hitting his palm.

The bodies of her brothers began bristling on the couch and Naomi prepared to dive in front of the glass case of her figurines. However, before she could move, Ethan planted himself in front of the curio cabinet and scowled at her family.

Arms crossed, he growled. "What did I say about behaving while in Naomi's house? Do we need to go somewhere to *discuss* this?"

Heads dropped, and the tension level in the room receded. Naomi gaped in astonishment at Ethan who nodded at her. "Come and eat, baby. We can't solve anything on an empty stomach and you've had a harsh day."

"But we've already eaten," Mitchell replied in a sulky tone.

Ethan's head swiveled and he fixed her brother with a dark glower. "I wasn't talking to you."

Laughter erupted and Naomi looked over to see her father bent over with mirth, slapping his leg. "Oh," he gasped. "Your mother was right. You don't need us here. Come on boys, let's go home."

"But—"

"How come—"

"Hey—"

"Now!" Naomi's father barked and her brothers stood with sullen looks. They filed out the door, with Chris tossing back a, "No fair. I wanted to kick some ass, too."

Her father beckoned and Naomi went to him for a hug. She snuggled her face in his plaid shirt, his Old Spice scent a familiar comfort. He kissed the top of her head. "I'm glad you're safe, baby girl, and it's about time you found some decent men to take care of you." With those words, her dad took off briskly.

"What? Hey, I can take care of myself," she yelled to her retreating father's back. He just waved in reply.

Slamming the door, Naomi whirled to find Ethan and Javier gone. Following the smell of food—Chinese, her favorite—she located them sitting at her kitchen table, ladling food onto plates. How utterly domestic and at the same time sexy.

Sliding into a seat, she thought about telling them to leave, but hunger—and a stupid girly happiness at their presence—won out. Besides, she couldn't eat all this food alone. They'd bought enough for a small army.

In between bites of chow mein, she eyed Ethan with curiosity. "How did you get them to behave? I kind of expected to see that a tornado had passed through."

"I wasn't going to let them get rowdy in your house. I told them that either they sat and waited, or we'd go to the gym right that second and I'd work off my anger issues."

"And they listened?" she asked.

Ethan shrugged. "I can be persuasive."

"Just who are you? Aliens?"

Javier choked and Naomi whirled to fix him with narrowed eyes.

"Whatever do you mean, baby?".

"Knowing what happened to me, my brother's should have been raving lunatics, destroying things left and right, venting. Instead, they were all prim and proper. Did you drug them?"

Javier spat out his water and Ethan chuckled. "Your brothers can act civilized. They just need reminding."

"Well, whatever you did, thank you. I don't know what I would have done if my butterflies had gotten trashed the same day as my car." The reminder of her Miata's demise soured her mood and she pushed food around on her plate.

"Don't worry about your car. The important thing is you're uninjured. Dessert?"

Naomi scowled. Why did they keep ignoring the fact she'd been victimized? At least her brothers wanted to hunt something down and kill it. Her supposed mates? They stuffed their faces, as if oblivious.

Isn't that what you wanted? Nice, normal human reactions. You should be happy your home survived a visit from your family, instead you're complaining because no one's roaring death threats.

Their lack of impulsive action should have pleased her. It didn't. She slid off her chair and paced. "Why are you both acting like my car getting trashed and my getting threatened is no big deal?" She blurted her thought out, and in the process of clearing the Chinese food, two sets of distinctly male eyes rotated to meet hers.

"Oh, we care alright," Javier replied softly.

"The asshole who did this will pay," Ethan rumbled.

"But don't worry," Javier continued. "We'll take care of this out of your sight so as to not upset your delicate sensibilities."

"You won't even hear them scream," Ethan promised.

It took her a moment to grasp their serenely spoken threats. "So you are pissed?"

"Of course we are," scoffed Javier. "But that doesn't mean we can't contain ourselves."

"Control, baby. We told you we had it. A prime example is how I didn't smack your brothers around when they arrived frisky and spoiling for a fight."

Javier turned to Ethan. "Dude, do you realize what this means?"

Ethan turned chocolate eyes, alight with smoldering lust her way. "It means we handled her family, and this situation, without violence."

"But you're planning on getting physical," she said, backing up even as a fire lit in her lower belly.

"As we said, you won't see or hear a thing, which meets the terms of the bet," Javier replied circling the table to the left. She whirled to flee via the other side, but Ethan already stood there.

"Don't tell me you're a sore loser," he chided. "This is one case, where being the loser is a win-win situation."

She thought about protesting more—maybe a little kicking and biting as foreplay—but her body betrayed her. Her head tilted back as Javier's hands slid around her middle from behind while Ethan crowded her from the front, towering over her.

"So you concede you lost?" Javier whispered in her ear before tugging at the lobe with his teeth.

"For now," she gasped as Ethan cupped her breasts, his thumbs brushing over the peaks. Even through the thin silk of her blouse, it felt like he branded her. Moist heat invaded her cleft and her legs trembled.

"Here or upstairs?" Ethan asked.

"Where do you usually eat dessert?" Javier replied.

Their intent caught her breath as they hoisted her onto the dining table. With two sets of hands, her clothes went flying in record speed, not that she could protest with Ethan's mouth plastered to hers. He kissed her and she forgot everything except the burgeoning pleasure in her body. While Ethan's lips clung to hers, caressing them, Javier also did his part, kneeling on the table behind her, his hands sweeping her hair aside to plant hot kisses on her nape. Shivers ran down her spine as he located her sensitive spots and sucked them.

But their mouths weren't the only busy things. Their hands roamed her body, tickling her skin with their rough texture, rasping along her tight nipples, stroking across the soft roundness of her belly.

Ethan's body pressed against her thighs, which spread wide to accommodate him. He inserted his still clothed body between them, the hard bulge at his groin pressing against her cleft. Firm hands gripped her about the waist and held her while he rubbed against her. Moisture pooled in her sex along with intense arousal. She panted against his mouth and soft mewling cries escaped her. She clung to his broad shoulders, her fingers digging into the hard muscle as her pleasure built at their simple, yet erotic, touches.

Ethan tore his mouth from hers and she made a plaintive cry. She opened eyes heavy with passion to see him looking at her with a torrid expression and kiss-swollen lips.

"You are so beautiful," he growled. Then he knelt so that she could only see the top of his head and she shuddered. She knew what he planned to do to her, and her cleft quivered in anticipation.

However, he teased her, rubbing the bristle on his jaw along the soft skin of her inner thigh. His warm breath brushed against her pussy. She almost forgot him as the body holding her upright at her back shifted and Javier lowered her torso to lie on the cold tabletop.

Then, she didn't even notice the chill surface because they both latched on to her body with a suddenness that made her exclaim and arch.

She couldn't have said which felt better. On the one hand, Javier's mouth tugged and sucked at her nipples while his hands kneaded them, the jolting pleasure travelling straight down to her pussy. On the other, Ethan's tongue, swiped up and down her cleft, lapping at her moisture, and delving between her lips.

Apart, they would have felt fantastic; together, they were incredible. Panting cries echoed in the room. *I'm the one yelling,* she vaguely noticed as her bliss built with each stroke and caress of their mouths and tongues. Intense heat boiled in her and need rode her body hard, yet still they tortured her. Her orgasm tore through her with startling suddenness, making her shriek, but they continued to caress her, their oral tease not finished.

Ecstasy built again in her sensitized flesh and hung there. She thrashed as they held her on the peak, her whole body vibrating with need.

"Fuck me," she cried.

"No," Javier whispered against her scorching skin. "Not until you accept us as your mates."

"Ethan, please," she begged too lost in the pleasure to care. Needing one of them to sink inside her and cure the burning desire inside her.

"Sorry, baby. I have to agree with Javier," Ethan replied in a ragged tone. "But don't worry, I won't let you suffer." He thrust two fingers into her, their length enough to touch her g-spot. Thrusting into her sex while flicking her clit with his tongue, Ethan threw her over the edge and Naomi screamed, a sound caught by Javier's mouth. She clung to his shoulders as she opened her mouth wide, her tongue plunging wetly into his mouth as her body shuddered with aftershocks that left her limp.

Javier kept his lips latched to her somehow as they scooped her off the table and carried her upstairs. Only when her back hit the bed did the kiss finally end. She opened eyelids heavy with spent passion to regard them.

Still dressed, if rumpled looking, Ethan and Javier stood at the foot of the bed, the evidence of their arousal packing quite the bulge in the crotch of their pants.

Sated didn't mean fully satisfied apparently, Naomi realized, as a tingle ran through her, making her catch her breath. *I want them to fuck me. I want them to sink their cocks inside me and pump me until I come all over them.* Just the thought made her quiver and she saw they'd caught her response because Ethan swallowed hard and Javier's eyes smoldered.

"Aren't you *coming*?" she wantonly asked.

"Not in you yet, we aren't, or have you decided to accept us as mates."

Naomi pouted. "Can't we just have great sex and not get into the whole bite-me and own-me for life thing?"

Javier shook his head.

Ethan didn't look happy about their stance, but he held firm in more than one way. "We don't want you just for the night. We want forever."

Irritated that they could refuse her—and annoyed that her wolf howled for her to give them what they wanted, what she stubbornly also wanted, but refused to admit—Naomi scrambled under her blanket. "You guys suck."

"Yes, we just did. And we can't wait until you can reciprocate."

Naomi nearly went cross eyed at the thought, but they weren't done teasing.

"Have you ever had two men at once?" Javier asked. She shook her head and a smile spread across his face. "Oh, sweetheart. When you do finally accept us, we are going to give you so much pleasure. Tonight will seem like nothing when we take you as we desire. Both of our cocks nestled inside your body, filling you up and fucking you until you come screaming. And as you thrash and claw at us, we will continue to fuck you, our bodies pumping in rhythm until you come again, and again."

Heart pounding, pussy dripping, she just about begged them to do it. To mark her and take her. And, she might have too had the phone not rung.

Ethan frowned and Javier muttered a low curse.

That quickly, the spell was broken, but even as she reassured her mother she was fine, she couldn't stop thinking of it.

Javier closed the bedroom door to give Naomi privacy while she spoke to her mother. He grabbed his cock and shifted it in his pants, a move aped by Ethan.

"Dammit, how much longer are we going to suffer, Javier? You heard her downstairs, she wanted us."

"She wanted out cocks. We need her to want our hearts and souls." What a change from a few days ago when all Javier thought he'd ever need was a warm pussy to sink into.

"I still don't see how torturing ourselves is helping," Ethan grumbled as they headed back downstairs.

"By showing her that her needs are more important than ours, we are laying the foundation for trust, my friend."

"Whatever. Trust won't matter if our dicks fall off first."

"If that happens, then we'll become oral experts. I wouldn't worry though. I don't think it will be much longer. Haven't you noticed? She's not threatening us or cussing us out as often. I think she's starting to like us."

Ethan chuckled. "But I like it when she cusses us out. It makes her even hotter and sexier."

"Don't worry, I'm sure we'll have plenty of occasions to set her off," Javier replied dryly. Truthfully, he liked Naomi's fiery side too. It made the women he'd known in the past pale in comparison. Forget someone who wanted to suck up to him, figuratively and literally. He wanted a woman who knew what she wanted, went after it and wasn't afraid to stand up for herself. A woman like Naomi.

Ethan tidied up the rest of dinner while Javier went out to the car and grabbed his laptop. When he came back in, Naomi stood in the kitchen wearing a robe and scowl.

"What do you mean you're spending the night?" she growled.

Javier bit his tongue as he tried not to grin at her bristling posture. Ethan was quite right—*she is hot when she gets like that.*

His friend stood his ground in the face of her annoyance and Javier could see his protective instincts coming to the fore. "Someone attacked your car. I am not leaving you alone to defend yourself."

"I don't need your help." She crossed her arms over her chest in a provocatively defiant gesture.

"Too bad, sweetheart," Javier interjected. "This is one case where you will not win. If it makes you feel better, we will sleep on the couches." Although, he truly hoped she'd shoot down that plan and invite them into her bed. Even cramped as it would be with the three of them—shopping for a new bed was a definite priority— holding her in their arms would make the discomfort of it worthwhile.

"Fine. Whatever. But don't expect me to make you breakfast," she snapped, perching herself on a stool at the kitchen island.

Ethan grinned. "Finally, a flaw. You can't cook."

"Can too," she retorted. Then she grinned back. "So long as you don't expect it to be edible."

Chuckles lightened the mood as Ethan set the dishwasher and Javier wiped down the counter. They'd both noticed her penchant for cleanliness and thought it best they do their part right from the start so as to give her less to argue about.

A bottle of wine emerged from the fridge and Ethan uncorked it, pouring them each a glass. Holding her goblet by the stem, Naomi shook her head. "Good grief. Did my mother leave me any secrets? My favorite wine. Food. The key to my house. What's left?"

"Well, we still don't know if you spit or swallow."

"Maybe she's one of those elusive garglers."

"Forget I asked," she mumbled, but she couldn't hide the pink stain in her cheeks or the quirk of her lips.

Javier and Ethan each snagged a stool across from her. It gave her space, but at the same time, gave them a perfect frontal view.

"Now what?" she asked, eying them a tad nervously.

"Now we discuss what happened today. Any idea who vandalized your car? And where's the note?" Javier asked.

"How do you know about the note?"

"Your father thankfully had the sense to not keep things from me. So spill it." Javier fixed her with a stern look. She didn't squirm or shy away as she had with the sexual innuendo. Instead, she flashed him her middle finger.

"I don't see why I have to tell you anything at all."

"Humor us," Ethan rumbled.

"Fine. There was a note. Happy. It wasn't signed. It didn't say much other than back off."

"Back off from whom?"

She shrugged.

"Did you give the cops the note?" Javier asked holding back a sigh of impatience.

"Yeah about that. I didn't call the cops."

"Why weren't they called?" Ethan asked in a deceptively calm voice.

Naomi shrugged. "And let them impound my baby as evidence? No thanks. Besides, we all know if the culprit is a shifter our version of justice will be more rapid and fitting."

Javier pretended to get shot and slapped a hand over his heart. "Wait? Did I just hear you advocating violence?"

Ethan chuckled.

Naomi glared. "Ha ha. So funny. I never said violence was never justified; there are occasions that warrant it. But I don't think it's too much to ask that some places, like my home, remain battle free zones."

"I'm just yanking your tail, sweetheart. Growing up, my mama had one rule—take it outside. Anyone who started something in her house learned real quick why you never messed with my mother." Javier raised his hand to his ear as if holding it and rolled his eyes.

The tinkling laughter almost upset him off his stool as Naomi finally relaxed enough to show them her softer side. "I think I'd like to meet your mother. Mine never seemed to mind the chaos. So long as they don't seriously hurt each other or dare to raise a hand to her, she doesn't care."

"But you do," Ethan added.

A shrug made the vee in her robe gape and it took some effort on his part to keep his gaze on her face instead of her shadowy cleavage.

"Unlike my mother, I like pretty things. Fragile things. I learned young though, owning something delicate wasn't feasible. It pissed me off. Still does."

"Why butterflies?" Javier asked. "I mean, I think we'd have understood if you collected wolves, but bugs?"

Naomi's head dropped but not enough to hide the color in her cheeks. Her fingers played with the stem of her wineglass. "You're going to laugh."

"I won't," Ethan assured. "And if the cat does, I'll put him out for the night."

A giggle escaped her. "Okay, well, here goes. It's kind of dorky. When I was a kid, I found a caterpillar. I hid him from my brothers in a margarine container and kept him under the porch. My first and only pet. I poked holes in the lid and filled the tub with branches and leaves just like the library book I had said to do."

"You like to read?"

Javier jabbed Ethan at his interruption. "Shut up and let her talk."

Naomi shrugged. "Yes, I love to read. I know, nerdy. But back to my caterpillar, I loved that thing. I'd lie on the grass and let him crawl on me, tickling me."

"What did you name him?"

"If you laugh, I will rip your balls off," she warned with a glare. She sighed. "Squirmy."

Javier chomped on the inside of his cheek to not laugh, and Ethan took a rapid sip of wine that he then choked on. Javier used that as an excuse to pound on his back.

Arms, crossed, Naomi watched them with one arched eyebrow. "Are you done yet?"

Composed again, Javier nodded his head.

"One day, when I looked in the container, Squirmy was gone and there was this chrysalis in his place. Oh, how I watched it." Naomi's lips curved into a sweet smile of remembrance, and her eyes took on a faraway cast. Javier's heart melted. "I waited what seemed like forever to see if he'd ever come out again. I didn't want to miss it." Her face fell and Javier knew they'd reached the crux of the story. "My brothers found my container first and played keep away with it. The lid popped off and scattered its contents. I screamed and cried."

"How many bruises did you give them?" Ethan asked.

A feral grin lit her face. "Enough that they learned not to mess with me, but it didn't bring back Squirmy. I was so upset. I still remember lying on my belly on the grass, days later, sniffling like a cry baby, when something with the most beautiful colors landed on my hand." She raised shining eyes to look at them. "My caterpillar, well, butterfly at that point, came back and it was so beautiful. My brothers hadn't killed Squirmy, even though he was so fragile. The only thing of mine I ever remembered not getting destroyed in one of their brawls. Of course, I couldn't keep it. It needed to fly and be free, but after that, I started collecting anything with butterflies. I drove my family quite nuts with it. In my teens I focused on the glass ones with the colored wings. Unfortunately, unlike my real one, they didn't all survive. But it didn't stop me from collecting."

"And believing that even amidst chaos, beauty can survive," Javier murmured.

"Kind of like you," Ethan said drawing the correlation. "A delicate flower amidst bumbling beasts."

Again, color heightened her cheeks. "I guess. I'd never thought of it that way. I just like them."

Ethan stood and left the room, returning with a box. He placed it in front of Naomi. She stared at it, not moving to open it.

122

"I don't need presents." She said, but Javier could almost touch the longing in her voice.

"Open it," Ethan urged. "Please."

"I'm still not letting you mark me," she warned as her nimble fingers untied the bow adorning the present and lifted the lid. "Oh."

She lifted out of the box, a butterfly with stained glass wings of amber shot through with gold hanging on a fine silver chain. Holding it up by the chain, she let it spin in the light, her eyes suspiciously damp.

"It's supposed to hang on the pulls for your ceiling fan. I thought you could put it on the one in your bedroom," Ethan explained. "And I promise you right now, no matter what you might think of us, what fears you might harbor, we will never, ever do anything that will break it."

"We won't let your treasures be broken, not by us or anyone else."

"I can't—You can't—" The words got caught in her throat and tears made her eyes shine. She fled the kitchen, the butterfly still clutched gently in her hand.

Ethan stood, but Javier put a hand on his arm. A fine tremble went through Ethan's body. "How can she be so feisty, yet so soft and girly at the same time?" he complained.

Javier smiled faintly. "Because she is perfect."

* * * * *

Curled on her bed, Naomi cradled the glass butterfly in the palm of her hand. It was absolutely gorgeous, and even worse, thoughtful. The idea that Ethan had actually gone into a novelty store selling such girly items as glass butterflies warmed her. It seemed so incongruous given his size and athletic profession. And yet, both he and Javier kept showing her other sides to themselves, gentler sides imbued with intelligence and respect. A respect for her and her wishes she'd never imagined with her own kind.

Instead of acting like cavemen and slinging her over their shoulder to have their wicked way with her— which admittedly would probably be lots of fun—they listened to her and followed her—sometimes irrational— dictates. They were turning out to be better than human options, the jerks.

Her resolve to never settle down with another shifter was melting rapidly beneath their determined assault. And after this evening's wicked orgasms, she found herself more tempted than ever.

But still, could she do it? Tie herself to not one, but two, dominant shifter males. Her inner conscience sassed, *Why not? They are, after all, the first two men I've met who, despite my occasional rude outbursts, still are determined to treat me like a fragile flower.* Of course, if she did decide to take them, she'd have to make them understand that sometimes a little man handling was allowed. Make that expected.

However, with her body still glowing from orgasm, her mind still whirling from the thoughtfulness of their aid this evening and the gift, it wasn't the time to make momentous decisions. Besides, she was kind of curious to see how much teasing they could take before one of them gave her what she wanted—a good hard fuck—without the benefit of a mark.

As she hung the butterfly on the hanging chain of her overhead light and fan, she pondered just what she could do to get them to melt at her feet. Or even better, melt inside her. Tired, a little lonely for someone

to cuddle, she laid down and let herself drift off, anxious
to set her plan in the motion the following day.

Chapter Eleven

She liked it! The knowledge he'd chosen well warmed Ethan as he stared down at Naomi while she slept. The present he'd agonized over in the tiny shop—which he'd feared tripping in and creating a catastrophe—hung on a chain and swirled with the air currents. When Javier had told him to pick something up that would cheer her, he'd immediately thought about her collection. After hearing her story, he congratulated himself silently on making the right choice and fell in love even deeper.

Some people scoffed at the notion of love at first sight. In the case of shifters, some argued that the mating instinct should not be confused with the emotion. However, while the mating instinct initially drove him to seek her out, everything he'd discovered since enchanted him about her. Now, several days since their first disastrous meeting, he was truly and completely in love with the feisty hellion who hid an inner softness, which made the fact she'd faced danger all the harder to bear.

His rage when he'd heard of her mishap had died down, but his beast still simmered below the surface, waiting for its chance to wreak vengeance at the one, or someones, who'd made Naomi sad. Ethan loved her courageous spirit, her seductive teasing side, her take-no-shit attitude, but he'd hated and felt helpless before her despondency. *Someone will pay.*

Brushing his lips feather light over her temple, he fought an urge to lie beside her when her lips curved into a sweet smile as she slept. Business first, though, cuddling later.

Ethan left the room and closed the bedroom door carefully before he went back downstairs. "She's sleeping," he announced quietly. "Did you find anything out?" His best friend, a lady's man and agile lacrosse player in public, turned techno geek behind closed doors.

Javier peered up from his laptop. "One possibility so far in her recent emails. Seems she might have stumbled onto a client misappropriating funds."

Flexing his fingers into fist, Ethan grinned. *Finally, someone he could vent on.* "Give me his address."

Javier snorted. "Why do you get to have all the fun?"

"Because one of us needs to stay here and guard her, or do you really think we should just wander off on a possible goose chase leaving her alone?" Ethan replied sarcastically.

"Good point. I'm surprised I didn't think of it first." Javier delivered the pompous claim with a grin.

"You probably didn't think of it because your balls aren't used to getting so little use. All that stemmed up jizz is affecting your brain power," Ethan retorted. Javier took aim with a sofa pillow, but Ethan held up a finger and wagged it. "Bad kitty. Naomi will kill us if she thinks we did anything to mess up her place."

"Since when are you the calm and collected one?" Javier growled.

"Since I got to taste the sweetest honey a bear could ever ask for."

Javier groaned. "Lucky bastard. Next time, I get the honey and you get to suck her succulent berries. I swear she almost came when I bit down on them."

Mmm, berries.

They both stopped talking and looked up at the ceiling, thinking of the woman asleep upstairs.

127

"You should go and question the guy. You're better at gleaning information. I'll stay and do guard duty." Ethan sighed in mock resignation.

Javier's eyes narrowed. "I can't let you sacrifice yourself like that, my friend. I'll stay, you go."

Ethan glared at his friend. "No. I insist."

"We'll flip for it."

"Fine. Heads, I stay and keep Naomi company while you go question suspect number one."

Javier lost, which totally pissed him off, Ethan judged by the scowl he tossed his way. Of course, it probably hadn't helped matters when Ethan had ribbed him saying, "Don't worry, I'll keep her *warm* until you get back."

Ethan deserved the shot to the gut Javier laid on him, but being the bigger man—especially between the legs—he grinned and mimed holding a pair of hips for fucking. Javier left with a disgusted snort and Ethan, with a chuckle, went back upstairs to check on Naomi. He discovered her tossing in her sleep, the scent of her arousal strong.

Dreaming of us, I hope. Actually, on second thought, she'd better be.

Carefully, he eased into her bed, the springs creaking ominously at his weight. He rolled her into his arms, enjoying the soft feel of her against him. His cock throbbed something fierce, but he ignored the ache. He knew the moment when he'd finally sink himself into her silken depths fast approached. Besides, in his mind—and even his bear's—all that mattered was making Naomi happy. Seeing her smile. Touching her. Tasting her. Feeling her come apart as she climaxed was well worth the agony of waiting for her to come to the conclusion she wanted them as mates.

128

And once she does finally get on board, I am going to plow her sweet body, again and again. Hell, I might just take up permanent residence between her legs. I can't wait until she's mine to love forever.

* * * * *

Naomi stretched in her bed—alone. Strange, because she could have sworn, she'd ended up pillowed between a pair of male bodies at one point during the night. Even more miraculous, they hadn't attempted to molest her. The jerks.

Surprisingly enough, she didn't find herself annoyed the guys had stayed the night in some sense of misplaced chivalry. It was kind of hard to remain irritated after the extreme pleasure they'd given her after dinner. It still blew her mind they'd expected nothing for themselves in return even though she saw the evidence of their turgid desire.

Worse, she almost wished she'd begged them harder to take her last night and mark her just so she could feel their cocks inside of her. Actually, in the light of day, she still had that urge. The mating call or lust, whatever she wanted to call it, rode her, making it difficult for her to keep recalling the reasons against binding herself to them.

A prism of light caught her eye and she looked up to see the morning sunlight making her butterfly shine brilliantly. She sighed. How could she keep fighting when they kept rendering themselves so utterly perfect and thoughtful? *If only they'd do something to piss me off.* Then again, given her current mood, she'd probably find any bad trait endearing at this point.

Springing out of bed, she headed into the bathroom for a hot shower. The simple act of washing herself proved titillating as each cleansing stroke of the soap woke her sensitized nerve endings. Ripe for sex, her body had never felt so alive.

When she emerged—hornier than hell—a warm fluffy towel awaited her along with Ethan's scorching gaze. Somehow, after the way they'd stripped and pleasured her, modesty seemed ridiculous. She stepped into the towel and let him wrap her in it. He rubbed her briskly, his eyes downcast as he patted every inch of her dry, well, except for the wettest spot. That area he avoided, to her chagrin.

Done, he stood and smiled down at her while giving her a bear hug that made her gasp.

"Good morning," she squeaked.

"Hey, baby," he rumbled, his soft brown eyes gazing down into hers. It seemed only natural to stand on tiptoe and tilt her head for a kiss. How far she'd come in one night and what a glorious way to start her day. Fire kindled low in her belly, and she moaned against his mouth.

Ethan pulled away and chuckled. "Come on, my hungry wolf. I've brought you breakfast."

Hunger of a different sort made her bold. "Who says I'm hungry for food?" Her sassy retort made him stumble on the way out of the bathroom and she slid up against his back, wrapping her arms around him to splay her hands flat on his rock hard stomach. "Actually, I can think of something I'd like to nibble on, but it doesn't rhyme with Danish."

A shudder went through his body. His large hands, almost paws given their size, came to rest atop hers. "You know mine and Javier's stance when it comes to sausage. Is this your way of saying you're ready to take the next step?"

No reply slipped from her lips even though her wolf howled "Yes!" in her mind. Wet, and her body afire for his touch, she didn't give up quite yet. Naomi slid around his body and sauntered to the bed, dropping the towel on her way. She heard him swallow hard and smiled. "Spoilsport. Why can't we just have a little fun?" An evil impulse overtook her and she bent over to open the bottom drawer of her dresser.

She never got a chance to straighten up.

"I can only take so much," Ethan muttered, his hands stroking over the skin of her ass. A finger dipped into the crevice and stroked her, and Naomi's knees trembled. She moved to bend up, but his hand pushed her back down before spanning her hips. Anchored, he thrust his jean covered groin against her exposed cleft.

Naomi moaned and pushed back against him. "That's it. Give it to me."

A sharp slap on her buttock made her yelp.

"Naughty wolf," Ethan growled moving away.

Rubbing her posterior, she turned to scowl at him. "Hey, what happened to treating me like a delicate freakn' flower?"

Ethan, his thumbs hooked in his jean pockets, gave her a smoldering look that made her cleft tingle. "That didn't hurt, and it was well deserved. You're teasing me. Trying to get me to do what you want."

"And the problem with that is?" she asked stepping into her panties slowly, knowing he watched her every move avidly.

"Fuck this."

In seconds, Naomi found herself flat on her bed, panties discarded. Ethan's body pressed between her

131

thighs as his mouth latched onto hers. She clung to him eagerly, letting her lips part so that their tongues could duel. He rubbed his jean clad cock against her mound, the rigidity of his shaft evident and fueling her desire. She mewled against his mouth, and he pumped against her.

"Ethan," she gasped.

He lifted himself to his knees, but kept his upper body bent over so as to not break their kiss. Her hands reached for him, but he remained out of reach. He, however, had perfect access. His rough fingers found her clit and stroked. She almost bit him as she arched up in pleasure. Faster and faster, he circled her nub while her panting cries grew louder.

"Oh, Ethan. Please," she begged as her body hung on the edge of bliss.

"I've got to get to practice," he whispered against her lips. "Get dressed." And then he moved off of her, taking his fingers and delicious mouth with him.

"What?" Her eyes wouldn't focus and her body burned.

"We both need to get to work. Come on, baby. We wouldn't want to be late."

"But…" She trailed off and looked at him, almost pleading for him to finish what he started.

"Next time you decide to tease me, make sure you're ready to take the punishment," he smirked, but his smoldering eyes betrayed his own lust. Not that the evidence of his own desire assuaged her.

Her mouth rounded into an "O" as anger suffused her. She bounced up on her bed. "You jerk. You made me horny on purpose. That wasn't nice." She snatched up a pillow.

He tsked her, wagging a finger. "Watch the butterfly, baby. I'm surprised at you. Really, violence because I made you hot and bothered? I thought better of you. Besides, you know what you've got to do if you want me to give you what you need. Just say the word, and I will be inside your body so quick, making you scream."

"That's blackmail," she yelled.

"I prefer to call it reality. You want it, then you've got to give me something in return."

Her cheeks burned because, in truth, she wanted them both. Wanted the excitement both mental and physical they brought into her life. Wanted them in her bed and inside her body. And her wolf wanted to mark them, bite them and show the world—especially all the skanky females—that they belonged exclusively to her.

However, she must have gotten dropped on the head one too many times as a child, because being given an ultimatum made her determined to do the opposite.

Taking careful aim, she fired the pillow at him. Then, she tackled him while he was distracted. Of course, her behemoth didn't budge, but she did enjoy how hands ended up cupping her buttocks and holding her against him while her legs wrapped around his waist.

"You don't play fair," she griped, glaring at him nose to nose.

"Neither do you," he replied. "It's one of the things I love about you."

His words threw her off balance—warming and yet panicking her. She decided she needed some distance as she cleared her mind. "You're a great big jerk for making me horny and not following through," she announced before jumping down. She stood with one hip cocked, still naked, and with nipples sharp enough to drill holes. "I'll get dressed, you evil bear, but just so you know, I always get even." She leaned up on tiptoe and kissed his chin, all she could reach, and copped a feel of his crotch, which made him grunt; however, not as much as she wanted to grunt when she felt the size of him. *Holy shit. That's one big bear.*

True to his word—and damned promise—Ethan made sure she got ready for work, driving her in a large, black SUV he owned. According to him, Javier had left earlier on some task requiring his attention. She hated to admit it, but she missed seeing him.

The drive didn't lack for conversation as it turned out Ethan enjoyed listening to the news on the AM channels and the question of the day debates. They got into a rousing discussion over the issue of whether or not the province should fund religious schools. To her delight, he provided interesting facts to back up his point, and before she knew it, they'd arrived at her work.

Silence fell as she prepared to leave him, something she found difficult. A part of her wanted to say screw work, to continue hanging out with him. Madness, and she squashed it by opening the truck door. As she prepared to hop out of his SUV, he leaned over, his big hand cupping the back of her head and drawing her toward him.

"Behave yourself, if you can, baby," he admonished with a smirk. "And call us if you need anything. Javier programmed your phone with our numbers." He kissed her, a slanting embrace over her lips that made her tingle from head to toe. "I'll see you after work," he growled, his eyes smoldering. "Javier will be coming by to take you to lunch."

He will, will he? Naomi stood on the pavement outside the office complex, her lips swollen, her pussy wet and a silly grin threatening. Apparently, she wasn't averse to taking orders, from her two jocks anyway. Anyone else who tried would get their face bitten off. Or, she'd report them to the Canadian equivalent of the IRS, which was actually much crueler.

What a letdown work proved after her titillating morning wakeup and distracting goodbye kiss. To keep herself from thinking of things she might pull off at her lunch with Javier, she checked her email, then voicemail.

George, her lawyer friend, still hadn't responded back, his last message still the brusque email to drop her investigation of the uncle's account. She dialed his office, which again went straight to voicemail, a full voicemail inbox. Unable to leave a message, she drummed her fingers on the desk, somewhat perturbed. Given the incident the previous day with her car, the fact her lawyer friend didn't answer or return her messages seemed ominous.

It occurred to her she could wander over to his office a few blocks away. Sure, Ethan had stressed the don't-go-anywhere-by-yourself thing, but really, didn't he know to whom he talked to? Nobody told her what she could do. Besides, someone would have to be foolish to try anything in broad daylight.

Before she could change her mind, she grabbed her purse and headed out.

"Josie, George isn't returning my calls, so I'm going to pop over to his office and have a chat with him."

"He's not there," Josie replied not looking up from her computer screen as she tapped away.

"How do you know that? Is he okay? Does anyone know where he is? When was the last time anyone saw him? Shoot, I hope he wasn't targeted as well," Naomi trailed off, wondering if she could call some shifter authorities.

Josie's fingers stopped typing and she looked up at Naomi, her blue eyes wide. "What the hell are you rambling on about now? There's nothing wrong with George. He happened to meet a woman, his mate, I might add. Turns out, she's the sister of the uncle you thought was screwing with the money. Speaking of which, I just got a FedEx package this morning with those missing receipts. Seems one of the little guys has been having a problem at school and the uncle's been setting up some private tutoring. Those receipts along with some others for some specialized equipment and drugs not covered by OHIP are in there. I was just typing them into the spreadsheet for you.

"Oh. So, George is alright?"

Josie rolled her eyes. "Well, duh, unless you think there's something wrong with boinking, like, a hundred times a day. I swear, you'd think they had some bunny somewhere in their gene pool. My cousin, who cleans his apartment, says the place reeks of sex and she's been washing sheets nonstop for the last two days."

Naomi's cheeks burned at the information, because she had to wonder, if she gave in to her own desires with Javier and Ethan, would she act the same way? *Like a bitch in heat. Awooo!*

Stepping back into her office, she slumped in her chair. A startling revelation—that didn't involve her hunk problem—made itself clear. *If the uncle is clean, who trashed my car?*

She didn't have the slightest clue. Nothing else in her recent dealings with clients appeared in the least shady, but maybe she'd inadvertently triggered some kind

136

of alarm. She'd have to go back through her files and see if she'd missed something.

The lunch hour arrived and Naomi found herself brushing her hair and reapplying lip gloss. Her girly reaction to the knowledge Javier would soon arrive to take her out made her want to bang her head off her desk—or even better, his hard stomach as she deep throated something long and hard. *Oh shit, I am in so much trouble. I don't know how much longer I can keep denying them. Denying myself.*

The fire in her sex, which had settled to a low burn, flared as she heard the rumble of Javier's voice through the door. Then he was there, filling her office with his scent. Her eyes devoured him in his casual jeans and button shirt, his hair still slick from a recent shower.

He held up a brown paper bag and smiled crookedly. "Sandwich delivery guy."

"How much do I owe you?" she asked in a husky tone she almost didn't recognize.

His eyes flared with heat. "One deep, prolonged kiss."

Naomi pushed back from her desk, the wheels on her chair scooting her away, and she beckoned him with a crooked finger, not completely in control of herself, and yet she couldn't entirely blame her wanton behavior on her wolf who yipped in anticipation. "Come and get it."

Dropping the bag on her desk, he moved to stand in front of her. Bracing his hands on the armrests of her chair first, he bent down until his face hovered just in front of hers. Impatient, and glad to see him after what seemed an interminable time, she grabbed his head and yanked him close enough for her to plaster her mouth against his. He held himself still as she slid her lips along his, her tongue teasing the part in them. With a groan, he dropped to his knees and his arms swept around her. Hugging her tight to his chest, she moaned in satisfaction. His mouth opened wide at her probing and his tongue swept into her moist recess, taking over the embrace and setting her on fire.

Enough sanity prevailed for her to gasp, "My secretary—"

"Has gone for lunch," he interrupted, dragging his mouth from hers to slide across the edge of her jaw. He planted rows of kisses on his way to her ear. "We really shouldn't be doing this, though."

"Now you sound like Ethan," she panted as he clamped onto her earlobe, sucking it and then swirling his tongue in the sensitive shell.

"Yes, he told me of your naughty behavior this morning before he left for practice. My poor little wolf. Are you feeling unwanted? Unfulfilled?"

"Yes. No." Her head tilted back to give him better access to her neck. He took advantage, blazing a trail down her skin.

"You only have to say the word, and we will give you everything your heart and body desires." He slid his hand up her skirt, his fingers dancing along her bare thighs to her damp apex. "Just give us permission to be with you forever and we will worship you with our mouths. Tease you with our fingers. And plow you with our cocks until you come screaming."

Talk about creating vivid fantasies. Naomi moaned as his fingers pressed against her core, tantalizing her with promised delights. His mouth left the soft skin of her neck to cover the aching peak of her breast, her nipple straining through the silken material for his touch. He bit down on it, and even with the fabric covering it, an electric jolt shot through her. She arched against him.

"Javier, please," she begged.

"Will you take me as mate?" he asked in a ragged voice.

"Would you accept a maybe?" And that quickly, he moved away leaving her bereft, cold—and horny.

"I brought you ham and cheese on a Panini. Light on the mayo with a touch of lettuce."

Through passion glazed eyes, she watched in disbelief as he opened the brown bag and pulled out food. If it hadn't been for the massive hard on he sported, she would have thought him unaffected.

"You guys aren't playing fair," she complained, trying to quell her wolf, which howled in her mind to pounce on him and bite. "Why can't we just fuck, and enjoy ourselves. Maybe this mating urge will wear off without the need to mark anyone."

Javier swiveled his head and shot her an incredulous look. "I know firsthand how a horny man can be stupid from a lack of blood to the brain, but I hadn't realized it extended to women."

Naomi flushed. "Are you calling me stupid?"

"Judging by what you just said, yes. That or really determined to ignore the truth. Can you honestly tell me you wolf doesn't want to claim me right now? To sink its teeth into my skin and leave a mark for everyone to see? To bind yourself to me?"

Naomi squirmed and scowled, especially since she currently fought the urge he just described. "But I don't want to. I want a normal, quiet life."

A snort escaped him. "Sweetheart, you aren't normal. But—" he held up his hand when she would have rebutted. "We can promise to do our best to keep the violence and chaos out of our home, unless you instigate it, of course."

"Are you implying I have a temper?" She arched a brow.

"That depends. Will you tackle me like you did yesterday? Because if you do, let me strip before I say yes, you have a formidable temper," he announced with a hopeful look on his face.

Biting her lip, she fought it, but lost. Giggles burst free. A moment later, Javier joined her. She grabbed a sandwich when her mirth died down and bit into it.

"Just because I'm not willing to take shit doesn't mean I'm not a delicate flower deep down inside," she informed him in between mouthfuls.

"The most beautiful flowers always have thorns."

They did, didn't they? "I'm still not crazy about it. I mean one shifter was bad enough, but fate is sticking me with two."

"Well, you could try bonding to only one of us," Javier said, mischief glinting in his eye. "But the one not chosen would probably try to drown his disappointment between the thighs of another."

Immediately, her wolf—and Naomi herself— bristled, as jealousy took her prisoner. Javier never saw the sandwich she flung in his face, but he sure felt it. Before he could wipe it off, she'd grabbed him by the balls and snarled. "Let's get one thing straight right now, my alley cat. There. Will. Be. No. Other. Women."

At Javier's pained grin, she growled. *Setup. Totally setup and I fell for it without a fight.* But still, it said a lot about her burgeoning feelings that even the mere thought of another woman with them would send her into a tizzy.

A beeping sound came from his pants and a chagrined look crossed Javier's face. "I must go. I've got a meeting to attend about Friday's match in Toronto."

"You're leaving town?"

"Yes."

"Oh." She tried to hide her disappointment at the knowledge. Sure, she'd gotten used to seeing them every day since the weekend, but that didn't mean anything. *Liar.*

Javier cocked his head and tilted her chin up. "Why are you looking so blue? Afraid you'll miss us? Don't worry, you're coming with us."

And that quickly, her despondency evaporated. Of course, she didn't let him know how happy his caveman claim made her. Instead, she harangued him for trying to control her, and making plans without asking.

But when he went to leave, she didn't fight him when he reeled her in for a kiss she felt all the way to her toes—and back up to her sex.

Chapter Twelve

Horny, but happy at how things were progressing, Javier left Naomi's office and met up with Ethan at the shifter's private sports complex. The big bear shook his head in silent reply at Javier's questioning look. Ethan had gone to talk with some contacts he had in the shifter underground to see if anyone might have heard anything about Naomi's attack, apparently in vain.

Damn. Another dead end to go with last night's visit to see Naomi's client. A total bust as it turned out the bamboozling uncle wasn't the car vandal.

Javier, in the hopes of gleaning some clues, had left early that morning—reluctantly from Naomi's bedside—and slipped into her office where he copied her hard drive onto a USB memory stick. The amount of info to sift through proved staggering, but they needed to find out who threatened her. The most logical explanation remained a client of hers trying to hide something. Finding out who was a task he'd tackle later. Right now, he headed upstairs for a team meeting and strategy session for their upcoming match in Toronto. A waste of time, Javier personally thought. He and Ethan would just do as they always did—plow through the opposition and win.

Ethan looked pensive as they took the elevator up to the war room. "You know, maybe it was just some random attack."

Javier's gut said otherwise. "How do you explain the note then?"

Ethan shrugged. "Maybe they hit the wrong car."

"Ah, yes, because there are so many other red Miata's in her parking garage," Javier replied sarcastically.

A glower pulled Ethan's brow down and he bared his teeth. "Smartass kitty. If you think you're so gosh damned smart, then why don't you come up with something, because I sure as hell haven't found anything that leads me to believe it'll happen again."

"Something doesn't smell right about it." And his inner cat agreed with bristling fur and soft growls. Their mate remained in danger.

"So we stick to her like glue. What a chore." Ethan rolled his eyes and chuckled. "I don't think there's a shifter stupid enough to try anything with us by her side."

Speaking of which, "I told her we were bringing her to Toronto with us."

"And? I see you have your balls still."

Javier grinned. "She called me a few names and accused us ordering her around, but she didn't say no."

"Think she'll let us mark her before then?" Ethan asked hopefully.

"My friend, I think short of a disaster tonight, nothing will stop her."

Fate had a bitching way, of course, of making people eat confident words.

A frantic phone call by an almost incoherent Naomi several hours later saw them racing in Javier's Lexus to reach her. They found her standing over her brother's bed at her parent's home. The young male appeared bruised and battered, but in good spirits judging by his toothy grins. His source of humor? His livid sister who cursed while she paced and recited in gruesome detail the damage she'd inflict on the ruffians who'd attacked him.

"How dare they!" she ranted. "Attack my little brother? The nerve! When I find them, I'm going to carve their testicles off and feed them to the birds. I'm gonna break every bone in their body, then run them over with my car. Wait, my car's broken. I'm gonna borrow a truck then, a big one and—"

Chris, the injured younger brother, rolled his eyes. "Thank fuck you guys finally got here. She hasn't stopped since she got here. Please tell my whack job of a sister to leave this one alone. As soon as I'm out of this bed, the boys and me are going to mete out some justice, wolf style." Chris grinned, his canine teeth showing.

"Ethan, please take Naomi downstairs for a drink of water. I think she's thirsty."

"Am not," she retorted.

"Ethan?" Javier gave his friend a look. With a nod, Ethan didn't bother arguing with Naomi, just scooped her up and threw her over his shoulder, caveman style. She, of course, shrieked and pounded at his back, but anchored by Ethan's thickly muscled arm, she couldn't escape. Screaming invectives that dwindled as they left, Javier sighed and turned to face Chris.

"You probably don't have long before she escapes him and comes back even louder than before."

"Thanks, man. I swear, I thought I was going to kill myself if she didn't shut up." Chris rolled his eyes.

"Your sister is understandably upset you were injured."

"Yeah, well, she'd be even more pissed if she found out if my beating was a warning to her."

His words froze Javier. "What did you say?"

"The four meatheads who jumped me were hired muscle. West coast boys judging by their accents. They took me by surprise coming off the college campus." Chris's face, the parts not purple and blue already, reddened with embarrassment.

"Those are bad odds for anyone, my friend."

Chris scoffed. "I betcha my sister's boyfriend downstairs wouldn't have even broken a sweat."

Javier inclined his head and smiled. "Yes, but he's special. Four would have been enough to take me out, though. What did they say to you to make you think this is related to Naomi?"

"It didn't make much sense. One of them grunted something like, 'Tell her to back off if she knows what's good for her' and the other said 'It would never work.' What the fuck is that supposed to mean?"

Puzzlement creased Javier's brow. "The mystery deepens." Before Javier could say anything else, movement at the door made him turn sharply. An ashen faced Naomi stood in the doorway. Ethan appeared behind her, his eyes stormy. He shrugged at Javier's look.

"They attacked you because of me?" she asked her brother in a quiet tone that made Chris blanch.

"Now, Noami, don't— "

"Don't what? Freak? Beat you for not telling me in the first place?"

"Uh, yeah."

Naomi whirled and moved to leave, but Ethan stood in her way. "Move or I'll hurt you again," she growled through gritted teeth.

Ethan's hand dropped to his groin and he moved aside.

"Ah shit, you better go after her," Chris groaned. "When she gets like this, you never know what will happen. Just don't get too close. She bites," he warned, followed by a muttered, "And she says we have a temper."

Worried now, he and Ethan tore down the stairs after her in time to hear a door slam shut.

"Where is she?" he asked.

The oldest brother, Derrick, shook his head. "She's gone out back to the woods. But I wouldn't recommend following."

"Come on," he urged Ethan, ignoring the warning as he skirted past her family who appeared to be planning something on the dining room table. The brothers appeared grim, but the father grinned like a mad wolf.

"Hot damn, Meredith," yelled Naomi's father. "Her beaus are gonna try and corral her while she's in one of her moods."

The muttered "Good luck's" weren't exactly reassuring. They exited the house via the back door in the kitchen, Meredith waving them through with a sly smile. They were in time to see the last of Naomi's clothing hit the ground before she called forth her wolf.

A rapid glance around showed nobody watching, but still…Javier hesitated to strip.

Meredith's soft voice came from behind him. "All the houses edging the woods are owned by folks who know. Your secret is safe here. Keep in mind, when you find her, she's gonna be pissed. Are you ready to handle that?"

Ethan already out of his shirt and working on his pants, grunted. "She's cute when she's angry. We can take whatever she dishes. She shouldn't be alone."

Javier joined Ethan in stripping, breathing out when Meredith left them. While nudity per say didn't bother him, the idea of stripping in front of Naomi's mother did.

Naked, he glanced over at Ethan. "She's gonna be faster than your bear. We'll handle this like we do in the game. I'll run her down and flush her back to you."

Ethan grinned. "Sounds good. My bear could use the exercise. See you in a few."

Quieting, Javier closed his eyes and called his jaguar. *Come on, old friend. Time to find our mate before she does something to hurt herself.*

His beast bounded forward in his mind and took over, reshaping his body and dropping him to four limbs. The change itself no longer hurt much, experience having taught him to accept his other half. In his cat form, he retained his sense of self and intelligence, but lost his ability to speak. He did however gain enhanced senses. And an urge to piss on everything, a part of the whole mark-the-territory thing all felines suffered.

Sniffing the encroaching evening air, the tantalizing scent of his female drifted to him. With a yowl, Javier sprinted off into the woods, the thrill of the chase firing up his adrenaline.

Wee little wolfie, kitty's come a hunting. And when I find my tasty treat, I think I'll have something good to eat.

* * * * *

Rage drove her to run. She needed to exert herself, expend the boiling anger at the knowledge that because of her someone had dared harm her family.

Cowards! She howled aloud, the sound echoing through the woods, a nature reserve set aside by the province to promote wildlife. And right now, given her turbulent emotions, she certainly counted.

To think, Chris thought to hide the reason of his beating from her. Trying to protect her. Idiot. They just didn't get it. She could handle herself and she didn't need them running interference for her anymore. She'd fight her own battles thank you very much. Now if only she could figure out whom she needed to kill.

The warning to back off just didn't make any sense, not without a name or another clue. She so desperately wanted an inkling, someone to turn her murderous focus on. Where she lacked the strength of a male, she made up for in deviousness. She wasn't stupid. She knew she couldn't tackle the problem face to face, but there were so many other wicked things she could do to tear their legs out.

Oops, did the bank freeze your accounts? What's that, did your credit card get reported stolen? Imagine that, someone repossessed your car and foreclosed on your mortgage. The financial world could be a vicious place for those who didn't know how to manipulate it. Then, once she'd crushed them, she would give the idiot to her brother.

Vicious plans didn't take care of her anger, though, only extreme physical exertion would, and maybe, if she was lucky, an encounter with wildlife that thought to get in her way.

As she leapt over a fallen tree, a tingling warning raced down her spine and brought her hackles up.

I am followed.

Slowing her headlong rush, she perked her ears, but heard nothing. A deep inhale brought her only the rich scents of the forest, her quarry downwind. *Friend or foe?* In her mood, she didn't really care. Peeling her teeth back from her gums, she stalked whatever dared interrupt her. The rustle of leaves proved her only warning before a large black shape soared from the darkness, its larger body, butting into hers and knocking her off balance. With a snarl, she whirled to grab a bite, but the shadow, feline in scent, leapt back into the gloomy woods.

Javier. She tore off after him, following the scent he no longer attempted to hide. But the jerk stayed just out of reach, his more agile body, clambering up trees then leaping from branch to branch.

Forced to navigate the pitfalls on the ground, she couldn't match his speed, and eventually, his limb to limb flight left her without a scent to follow. Not willing to concede to his beast, she kept foraging forward, nose to the ground sniffing.

An acrid stench made her wrinkle her muzzle. *Piss! The nervy cat marked our woods.* Naomi would have probably smiled if she'd worn her human shape. Her family and neighbors would probably have a conniption when they came across the big cat's territorial claim.

His trail evident once again as he kept to the ground, she followed Javier, his black fur blending so well in the darkness that she almost went right past him, only the flashing glint of his eyes alerting her to his presence.

Pulling her teeth back and curious to see how her wolf fared against the large cat, she lunged at him, throwing her body against his. Taking him by surprise, she managed to knock him over, and she got her teeth around his neck, biting with just enough pressure for him to lie still.

Gotcha, she thought.

So intent was she on her victory that she missed the movement behind her, but she caught the scent of bear. A roar split the night, and even guessing it belonged to Ethan didn't prevent her wolf from shivering, especially when she peered up and saw the size of him.

Towering taller than she'd imagined a body could stretch with thick fur, a heavily muscled frame, and great big teeth, Ethan was absolutely magnificent. And kind of freaky in a he-could-totally-kill-me-with-a-swipe-of-his-paw kind of way. She took a step back, then, sat hard on her ass when the great, big, scary bear waved a paw at her and grinned by pulling his lips back to show some teeth.

Her anger, having receded during her hunt of Javier, became completely replaced with mirth as the Kodiak bear sat down and cocked his head, looking like a cuddly teddy.

She shifted back and shook her head. "How's a girl supposed to stay pissed when you're acting like the world's cutest carnival prize?" she snapped, her rebuke tempered with a smile. Ethan lifted hairy paws and shrugged. Naomi couldn't help giggling. A furry head butted her from behind and she peered sideways to see Javier's slick feline shape.

She let her fingers rub the fur between his ears, the hair softer than expected. Mischief made her scrub him hard behind the ears while crooning, "Who's a pretty kitty? You like that don't you." A loud purring met her ministrations and she giggled. "Look who's a big suck. Oops, I mean ferocious man eating panther."

A snort from behind made her let go of Javier who sank to the ground rumbling. She crossed over to Ethan and wrapped her arms around his thick neck. "Jealous? Don't worry. I've always had a thing for bears. They're right after butterflies."

"Is that so?" Javier drawled from behind.

Naomi whirled and grinned. "Would it help if I said kitties came in a close third?" Her smile soon faded though as she realized something very important. Javier stood very naked in front of her, and he was *really* happy to see her. Apparently just as happy as the big body that brushed up against her back.

A step was all it took to bring Javier close enough for her to feel the heat radiating off his body. She tilted her head back and peered up at him, licking her dry lips as anticipation lit a fire in her stomach. "Why did you come after me? Didn't my family warn you, I'm a bitch when I'm in a mood?"

Big hands rested on the curve of her waist as Ethan rumbled. "I like you when you get all feisty. Besides, we weren't about to leave you alone."

"I can take care of myself." She just couldn't protect her family it seemed. Anger resurfaced with a vengeance. "I can't believe they went after Chris instead of me."

"They obviously know how much your family means to you," Javier replied, his fingers trailing across her cheek and down her neck, fusing her anger with her increasing desire.

"I want to hurt them," she growled.

"I know, sweetheart."

"Trust me, we want to hurt them too, baby" Ethan added.

"But in the meantime, you need to be careful. Running off alone in the woods, especially given what's been happening, may not be the wisest course of action."

Lips pursed and eyes narrowed, Naomi glared up at the voice of reason. "And how else was I supposed to work off my frustration. I couldn't go home in this condition. I need to vent."

"What happened to living a calm life?" Ethan teased, his thumbs rubbing circles on the skin of her waist.

"They hurt my brother," she whispered. Saying the words aloud brought home a very scary fact she'd not wanted to think of before. "They could have killed Chris," she yelled, her hands slapping forward against Javier's chest.

He caught her wrists and pulled them up. "There are better, just as energetic ways to take care of your frustrations."

"I thought sex was out unless I let you both bite me," she retorted.

"It is," Javier announced. "But I think we can give you relief in other ways."

Naomi almost said, screw it, bite me. She knew they could make her come, bring her to pleasurable heights. But she wanted more than that. She wanted them, inside her, marking her, claiming her. *Belonging to me.*

Why exactly did she fight them still? Sure, she'd known them less than a week, but in that time they'd proven they owned the qualities she looked for in a mate, plus some she would never have thought of. Did she love them? She wasn't sure yet. She knew her mother had mated to her father before she'd grown to love him, but as her mother confided, all the best relationships started with lust. Love was only something that came after time. And grew stronger the older it got.

The real question was did she dare take a chance on these two males? Males who kept proving in little ways they cared for her—temper, irrationalities and all? Who fired her blood and didn't fear her when she let loose?

Yes. Yes, I want them in my life. I want to get to know them. I want to fight with them and make up. I want them. The answer, once she admitted it to herself, made her feel light. She took a step out from between them, and took a breath, "I—"

A cracking sound made her halt. Splinters rained as something impacted the tree to the left of her. A moment later, Javier stood in front of her, his body flinching as another report sounded.

Naomi squealed as she found herself thrown to the ground, Javier's body heavy on hers as a roar shook the forest. With a growl to make any but the bravest piss themselves, she heard the crashing sound of a shifted Ethan lumbering off after the shooter.

Heart pounding, Naomi tried to catch her breath, fear and indignation battling for supremacy. *Someone shot at me!*

Warm moisture and the recognizable scent of blood made her eyes widen. "Javier? Oh, my god. Javier, were you shot?"

"I'm fine, sweetheart. The more important question is, are you unhurt?"

"Other than being squished, yes. But if you're fine, why do I smell blood?"

Shifting his body off of hers, Javier moved into a crouch, his eyes scanning the darkness. In the distance the occasional roar drifted to their ears as Ethan chased the hunter. Naomi sniffed the air, the scent of blood still strong. She reached out a hand and ran it up Javier's arms, encountering moisture.

"You've been shot!" she exclaimed.

"Bah, 'tis but a scratch," he scoffed.

"Are you seriously quoting *Monty Python* to me, you geek?"

His soft chuckle eased some of her tension. "Come on, you gotta admit, it works in this occasion. Or would you have preferred something more modern classic like 'Excellent.'" He doped up his voice, and Naomi bit her lips so as to not give in to hysterical laughter as he mimicked the idiot from *Bill and Ted's Excellent Adventure.*

She jumped up and stared down at him, her heart pounding. "I was thinking more along the line of what the hell were you thinking of acting like a human shield so you could take a bullet for me?" Naomi planted her hands on her hips and yelled at him. It was either holler or kiss him silly for doing something so incredibly courageous and dumb.

Standing, he peered down at her. "Is it too soon to say I would die for you?"

She slapped his uninjured arm. "Idiot." The word came out sounding like an endearment and he grinned.

"If you're done acting like a wife, can we head back to the house?"

"Are you trying to protect me again?"

"No. I need a Band-Aid and a beer, not to mention my man-parts are getting cold out here."

Naomi's gaze flicked down and took in his cock, lying limp amidst his dark curls; although, it didn't stay still for long. "Nice to see your blood loss hasn't affected your equipment. But seriously, you can't mean to leave Ethan out here by himself? Or have you forgotten there's someone with a gun?"

Javier grinned. "Worry about an Alaskan Kodiak bear? That's funny. I'm more worried about him not bringing any pieces back if he catches him. Ethan's going to be fine. Shifted, it would take more than a few bullets to stop him. He's built of good stock. You on the other hand, are a delicate flower."

Naomi stuck her tongue out at him in a childish gesture as he reminded her of her claim. *Jerk, he would use it against me.*

A growl rumbled in his chest. "Don't point that thing at me unless you intend to use it. Now come on, my lazy wolf. Shift your delectable ass so I can chase it back to the house." When Naomi would have argued some more just because it was fun, he slapped her on the behind, and not a light love tap. He cracked her hard enough to make her yelp. But did he stick around for retaliation? No, the jerk shifted and bounded off, followed seconds later by Naomi. And he kept his promise, nipping her bottom whenever she slowed to listen or look for Ethan.

The pandemonium when they reached house proved epic, especially once her family heard about the gunman. Naomi's brothers, with her father leading the way, poured out of the house, tearing at their clothes. Shifting into big, hairy wolves, they sprinted off into the woods, baying like wild animals. All except for poor Stu, who pulled the short straw and ended up with guard duty at the house.

Naomi's mother took one look at the deep gouge on Javier's arm and went for her first aid kit while Naomi blushed and tried not to look as he pulled his pants up over a cock that refused to stay down.

A part of her wanted to leave so she could join her brothers in the hunt—AKA ensure herself of Ethan's safety—and sink her teeth into the bastard who'd hurt Javier. However, worry for injured Javier and Chris, who only had Stu and her mother to guard them, made her stay inside. Of course, the idea of guarding Javier was comical. Other than the bandage, he looked perfectly capable, but she catered to him anyway, cuddling him on the couch after she fetched them both a beer.

Stupid or not, the damned cat did stop a bullet for me. It made her grudgingly like him even more. As for Ethan, right after she reassured herself he'd returned intact, she'd tear him a new one for rushing off by himself. Then she'd kiss him because, dammit, she couldn't help caring for him, too. *Stupid dumbasses.*

Cradled on Javier's lap, her head nestled against his chest, waiting for news, the steady thump of his heart lulled her and she fell asleep.

Chapter Thirteen

Ethan kept peering in the rearview mirror at Naomi, curled up and sleeping on the backseat. It had taken quite a bit of convincing to get her to agree to leave and come with them to Toronto. She'd kept insisting she needed to stay and protect Chris, who in turn yelled she was treating him like a little girl. And then, it degenerated even further when she played the world's tiniest violin.

They'd only managed to pry her from the doorframe, as she sang the refrain from "Cry Baby, Cry," by whispering in her ear that she couldn't play a crucial part in their plan to snare her assailants if she didn't come with them.

"Are you going to use me as bait?" she'd asked with narrowed eyes.

"Yes," Ethan had answered bluntly.

"I'm in," she'd chirped.

The process of packing her a bag and grabbing their stuff took some running around, but they finally got on the road to Toronto mid-morning and she'd promptly fallen asleep in the back of the SUV, using Ethan's sweater as a pillow.

"I'm not sure I like this idea," Ethan growled in a low tone, repeating his dislike of the plan for the umpteenth time.

Javier sighed as he drummed his fingers on the armrest. "We don't have a choice. You and I both know if we don't do something, and quick, Naomi's liable to do something rash."

Yes, she would, the cute little thing. "But still, couldn't we have just have handcuffed her to a bed in her parent's house while we hunted the bastards down?"

"I'd prefer to save the cuffs for some erotic fun. Besides, you and I both know if we tried anything like that she'd probably rip our dicks off."

A chuckle escaped Ethan and he glanced in the rearview mirror to peek on her again. "Fine. But, using her as bait? What if it backfires and she gets hurt?"

"Nothing will happen to her," Javier swore. "And the sooner we take care of this dilemma, the quicker we go back to wooing her. Speaking of which, I got us a suite with a king sized bed and an in-room hot tub."

"Nice. Remind me when we get back to do something about her damned tiny bed. It has got to go."

"When you replace it, make sure you get something with a headboard you can latch those handcuffs onto," murmured Naomi in a sleep tinged voice. "I've always thought bondage sounded like fun." Her husky chuckle made Ethan lose focus and the SUV swerved on the road.

"How much did you hear?" Javier asked, turning sideways to glance at her in the back.

"Enough," she replied, sitting up with a stretch. "Mmm. I've got to say, a hot tub sounds awful good right about now."

"Want me to climb in the back and give you a massage?" Javier offered.

"I can wait. I wouldn't want Ethan to feel left out." Her tone hinted at sensual delights which confused Ethan, who'd grown used to her prickly nature.

"You seem awful calm and relaxed. Shouldn't you be freaking out?"

"Or demanding your own room?" Javier added.

Naomi leaned forward, an arm propped on each front row seat. "Well, I've had some time to think. You know, you're both not bad, for shifters that is. I guess you could even say I like you."

"And?" Ethan queried. His hand gripped the steering column tight enough to turn his knuckles white.

"My body really likes you both, and my wolf is just dying to take a bite. So…" She trailed off, and Ethan ignored the road to turn sideways to look at her. Javier aped him and they both stared at her slow, impish smile.

"Sweetheart, you're killing us here."

"Oh, well, I was just going to say maybe, once we get to the hotel, we could strip off all our clothes…"

"Yes."

"Slip into the hot tub."

"Oh, yes."

"Javier, you'll rub my shoulders while my big, old bear here rubs my little feet."

"Naomi!" The warning in his tone made her smile wider and tired of splitting his gaze between the road and her, Ethan swerved onto the shoulder and slammed the SUV to a stop. The sudden halt flung her forward, but Javier caught her propelled body and dragged her onto his lap.

Ethan pivoted sideways in his seat and growled at the mischief in her eyes. "You're teasing us again."

She nodded her head, her sharp white teeth catching her bottom lip as if to contain her humor.

"Are you telling us you're ready?" Javier asked quietly before nuzzling the skin of her neck.

"If you mean after the body massage I expect you to lick and touch every inch of me, and then take turns fucking me as I mark you, then—"

She never did finish her sentence because Ethan swooped forward and claimed her lips possessively. He couldn't stop himself, not when she'd finally admitted she wanted them. *Wants me.* The taste of her made him groan; a sound repeated when she opened her mouth and let his tongue in to twine with hers.

Fire raced through his veins along with a desperate need to claim her. To leave his mark on her skin to show the whole world this delightful female had chosen him. And he in turn belonged to her, forevermore.

He left her delectable mouth to nuzzle the soft skin of her neck, and Javier took his turn, claiming her lips. Ethan's hands cupped the fullness of her breasts, his thumbs rubbing across her erect points, the friction of material not enough to mask the rising heat of her body. He could also smell it, her musky arousal, a potent ambrosia that made his mouth water for a taste. The windows of the truck steamed up as their arousal mounted.

The blast of an air horn from a passing semi-truck brought Ethan back to reality. He couldn't, make that wouldn't claim Naomi on the side of the road in full view of passing traffic. She deserved only the best, in other words, the woman they adored merited a bed—a soft surface where they could explore her body and bring her to rapturous heights before they marked her. *I want the moment we join to be memorable and beautiful.*

Ethan pulled away and she mewled in loss, her hands reaching out to clutch at him, to draw him back.

"Why are you stopping?" she murmured huskily.

"Our first time with you isn't going to be in a cramped back seat or on the hood of the truck. We will finish this when we reach a bed. Or at least a private room where we don't have to worry about an audience or cops showing up to give us a ticket for indecent exposure." he muttered, unable to resist brushing a knuckle across her straining nipples.

Javier's hooded eyes peered at him as he let off caressing her ear lobe. "Then we need to get to the hotel pronto."

"Can't we just recline the seats?" she asked breathlessly.

"Think of the next forty five minutes as foreplay," Javier replied. "Because once we get to the hotel, I don't know how much control we're going to have for round one."

"Just how many rounds are we going to have?"

"As many as it takes to make sure we can go at least an hour without a hard on," Ethan growled. "Now, get that delicious ass of yours in the backseat and stop distracting me, or I won't be responsible for what happens."

"Promises, promises," she muttered clambering into the back.

He couldn't resist swatting her ass and grinned at her yelp. "Naughty vixen."

Ethan floored the gas pedal, spraying gravel and got them on the road again. He hummed as he drove, a silly smile plastered to his face. He got the feeling he'd be smiling a lot in the next twenty-four hours, in between bellowing as he came of course.

* * * * *

The last hour of the road trip seemed to take forever, especially since they'd restricted her to the backseat. Naomi didn't take her banishment without a fight, though. Sitting there with her legs splayed, she pulled a Francine—who would have probably wiped a tear of mirthful pride—and whispered dirty things. Things that usually would have made her blush, but given her state of arousal just kept her primed. Nasty, yet truthful, words about what she wanted them to do to her, and what she intended to do to them.

"I'm going to get on my knees and see just how much of that giant cock of yours I can take in my mouth, my big bear," she whispered, her own words titillating her but not as much as the heated looks Ethan kept giving her in the rear view mirror.

To Javier—"Since you seem to love my tits so much, I'm going to lie on my back and you're going to slide that long prick of yours between them far enough that I can suck the tip."

Javier let out a noisy breath, but didn't turn to look at her. "Faster, dude, or I swear I'm going to jack off all over your nice leather seats."

Naomi barely noticed when they pulled into the hotel. In a flash, she found herself standing on the pavement as Ethan thrust his keys and some bills at the valet to park his SUV and bring in their luggage. Anchored to Ethan's side by his thick arm, she clung to him in a daze, her need to be with him and Javier overriding everything else. A part of her recognized that her shifter side—AKA the mating urge—was to blame for the urgency of her need, but another good portion of it just had to do with good, old-fashioned lust.

She'd fought her attraction to them for too long at this point. She could no longer deny, even to herself, that she not only wanted their bodies, but also the men themselves. How could she not when they seemed to understand her, to accept her as she was even with all her crazy idiosyncrasies. A heady feeling for someone who'd always assumed she'd have to hide her true nature in order to settle down.

As Javier checked them in, she dragged Ethan's face down for a kiss, but he only let her enjoy a brief taste before pulling away. She made a moue of disappointment, only somewhat mollified by his smoldering eyes.

"Just a little longer, baby. Javier's getting the key."

True to his word, in moments, she found herself ensconced in an elevator, sandwiched between them. Ethan dipped his head at her urging and let her claim his mouth. She took full advantage sucking on his lower lip and even nibbling it as Javier pressed in from behind, his groin, with his hard shaft, grinding against her ass. She molded herself to Ethan's front, her whole body afire at the sensation of being caught between them. *The only way this could get better is if we were all naked.*

Arousal peaking at that thought, she sucked Ethan's tongue into her mouth, and moaned at the electric sensation such an intimate kiss caused in her body. With a growl, Ethan lifted her off the ground and she wrapped her legs around his waist. Javier chuckled at her eagerness, a sound she felt against her bottom as he dropped to his knees in the elevator. Her position spread her cheeks and gave Javier access to her pussy, which, even clad in her jeans, felt the warmth of his breath as he blew hotly against it.

A bell dinged, and she clung to Ethan as he exited the elevator and strode down the hall. Her arms wound around his neck, toying with his short hair while her lips devoured his hungrily. A click sounded and she opened her eyes at half-mast to see they'd entered a spacious suite. She only had eyes for the large bed, though. Still wrapped around Ethan, his big hands now cupping her buttocks as he carried her, he lowered her backward onto the bed until she hit the mattress. Only then did she reluctantly release her hold on him.

Javier came to stand beside Ethan, and oh, how they took her breath away. Both so handsome in their own right, yet so different.

Thick and muscled with pale skin that tempted her to touch, Ethan towered over her, the solid strength of his beast—*my beast*—evident, and simmering below the surface. Yet she didn't fear him. She knew with all of her being, he would never hurt her; although, she didn't doubt he'd be ferocious in his defense of her. He perhaps lacked the suave actions and words of Javier, but in his simple, shyer way, he made her feel special and dainty, a unique feeling she cherished.

And then there was Javier. Slimmer of build and shorter in stature at just over six foot, his muscles were of the leaner variety, encased in smooth, tanned skin— lickable skin. He moved with the grace of his kind, a jungle cat, barely tamed, who flouted the usual feline 'love 'em and leave 'em' tradition because of his need for her, and only her. She'd initially feared she would just end up another notch on his infamous belt of conquests, but somehow, during the last week, she'd gotten to know him, to understand how strongly he believed in honor. When he gave his word, he kept it. She no longer feared giving herself to him. Once he committed himself to her, he also would never do anything to hurt her.

They both just wanted a chance to please her— and love her.

The knowledge awed and humbled her. It also fired up her erotic hunger and increased her need to claim them. To mark these men and make them hers.

*And most exciting—and scary—of all, to freely love them in
return.*

They watched her with fierce gazes, their lust for
her evident, but she could also see their affection. She
knew if she said no, even given their current state, they'd
respect her wishes and walk away. They wouldn't force
her. The first move had to come from her.

Sitting up on the bed, Naomi held their gaze as
she stripped off her shirt and unclasped her bra. Her
heavy breasts sprang free, and she cupped them with a
coy look.

"Any reason why you're not getting naked, too?"
she asked.

"Are you sure?" Javier replied. Ethan clenched
his jaw tight as he waited for her answer.

"Positive," she replied as she unbuttoned her
pants. She laid back and pushed them down over her
hips then their hands tangled with hers as they helped
her to remove them. Hooking her fingers through the
sides of her panties, she watched them swallow hard as
she took care of those as well.

Naked—and hornier than hell—she flashed
them a sensual smile. "Before you decide to interrupt me
again at an inopportune moment, let it be known right
now, I intend to claim you both. So stop staring and get
to work because I could have sworn you said round one
wouldn't take long and I'm really freakn' horny."

Funny how a few small words could get them to
tear off their shirts and shuck their pants. Denuded, they
revealed two hard and bobbing cocks. How decadent.
Wet heat gushed into her cleft, as her body prepared
itself for a wild ride.

A question crossed her mind as they both
clambered onto the bed, flanking her.

165

"So this might be a stupid question, but how is this going to work? I mean there are two of you and one of me."

"You have enough holes to take us both at the same time," Javier grinned, his hand stroking the length of his shaft, making her mouth water with hunger.

"You mean my mouth and pussy?" she clarified, trembling as Ethan stroked his hand up her thigh, brushing her curls.

Javier reached out a hand and tweaked her nipple before rolling it between his fingers. "Am I to assume you've never had a man in your ass?"

Actually, it had never occurred to her to try. She bit her lower lip and shook her head.

"We will save that for another night then. For now, Ethan and I shall take turns plowing your sweet sex. Filling you up with our essence and taking turns marking you. But soon we will introduce you to a true double penetration where I will get your sweet ass and my large friend here, will plow your pussy."

"At the same time?" Her eyes widened.

"We'll be gentle," Ethan promised, dipping his head down to stroke his mouth over the soft skin of her thighs.

She would have answered, but Javier took that same moment to swoop down and nip one of her nipples, making her cry out. His hot mouth sucked the erect tip of her breast, the tug somehow creating a direct sensual link to her pussy, which throbbed in reply. A moan escaped her as warm breath brushed her cleft as Ethan blew on it, teasing her. He flicked his tongue across her clit, and her pelvis arched in reply.

"Stop," she panted. "I'm too close to coming, and I want to save it for your cocks. You've made me wait long enough."

Two sets of mouths stilled.

"You're going to kill us," Javier moaned.

"At least I'll die happy," Ethan added.

Pushing up to a sitting position, Naomi decided to take control before she completely lost her mind. Besides, she owed them for driving her wild these past few days. "Oh, shut up and get on your back," she ordered. "Both of you."

With a quick look at each other, her men obeyed, rolling onto their backs on either side of her. Their cocks jutted from their loins. Javier's strained upward, long and curving while Ethan's stood almost as long but thicker, much thicker than she'd thought possible. *Oh my. That's going to be a tight squeeze.* Her channel quivered in anticipation.

"Hands behind your heads," she continued. Smoldering eyes met hers, but they complied, their stretched arms exposing their muscled chests to perfection. Excitement made her blood pump furiously as she enjoyed her power over them.

Seated between them, she reached out both hands and grasped each of their pricks, chuckling softly at the way they jerked in her grasp. Slowly, she stroked them, up and down, her tight fist feeling every nuance of their shape, and their pulsing arousal. She flicked her gaze back and forth between them, fascinated at the way their corded bodies tightened as they strained to control their desire. She didn't dare meet their eyes because she knew their heated gaze would burn her up.

Up and down, she shafted them, fascinated as their balls pulled up tight and their thighs clenched in an attempt to restrain themselves. Evidently, they were both more than ready for her, thank god, because she couldn't wait any longer.

She'd already decided to take Javier's shaft first, a warm up, so to speak, for Ethan's much larger cock. However, how did she make sure Ethan didn't feel hurt at her choice?

"Um, did you guys happen to decide beforehand who would go first?" she asked nonchalantly.

As if sensing her dilemma, Ethan smiled. "Take Javier first. I want you primed for my dick. And don't worry about hurting my feelings. I like to watch." He winked and she almost went cross eyed at his words. Somehow, she hadn't clued in that whatever she did with one would provide visual entertainment for the other. The idea titillated her.

Unable to wait any longer, she straddled Javier's hips, lowering herself just enough for the tip of his cock to nudge at her moist lips. She reached down and grabbed a hold of his prick, rubbing the swollen head against her clit. A shudder went through her as the pressure made her pussy clench.

"Sweetheart," Javier moaned apparently just as tortured by her sexy play.

"What's wrong, kitty, can't take a little teasing?" She ran his cock back and forth against her wet slit, her breath catching as she watched his reaction. His muscles tensed under her sensual tease and his eyes closed. Unfortunately, as erotic as he found her actions, it was tenfold for her and she couldn't keep it up.

Slowly, she lowered herself on his shaft, impaling herself on his length and unable to prevent her channel from gripping him convulsively in a pre-orgasmic quiver.

"Yes," Javier hissed, his hands finding and digging into her hips. Up he thrust, sliding his shaft the rest of the way home, a delectable move that made her cry out and throw her head back as she absorbed and enjoyed the sensation. It took her a moment to adjust to him and the fiery pleasure imbuing her body, but once she had, she wanted more.

Fully seated on his length, she splayed her hands on his chest and dipped her head forward, sending her long hair swinging in a silken curtain. Javier smiled up at her, a wicked curve of his lips that went well with the smoky desire in his eyes. She wanted to kiss those lips, to taste him on her tongue, but he reached up and tweaked a nipple. Then he pinched it, an intense sensation which made her pussy squeeze around his cock and made her reel with a gasp. She tried to regain control; however, he didn't give her time to recover. He gyrated his hips and she mewled as it put pressure on her clit. Her nails dug into his chest as she rocked in time to his subtle thrusts, the deep penetration striking a sensitive spot inside her, heightening the intensity of the moment.

From behind, Ethan's body brushed up against hers, his rough hands cupping her heavy breasts while his warm breath feathered her ear. He stroked a thumb over her taut peaks as he whispered, "Ride him, baby. Take him nice and deep." She moaned at the dirty words, grinding herself hard against Javier who groaned aloud. But Ethan wasn't done and he rolled her nipples as he continued to talk. "Squeeze his cock tight with that sweet pussy of yours. Fuck him, baby. Come all over his dick and cover him in your cream. And remember, once you're done milking his prick, I'm going to plow your still quivering channel with my big cock."

Never having indulged in dirty talk during sex before, Naomi nevertheless enjoyed it. Actually, she more than enjoyed it. Ethan's words heightened her arousal and she rotated her hips faster. Behind her, Ethan's cock rubbed against her backside as his hands slid to her waist and helped her rock at an even quicker pace. Her body tightened in pleasure, and then Ethan murmured. "Claim him, Naomi. Take him now as you come on his cock."

Up until that moment, her wolf had played the part of silent if eager bystander. At his words, her bitch bounded forward in her mind, wrestling for some of her control. Naomi, in the pre-throes of climax, felt her leash slip. She fell forward, her mouth opening wide and her incisors lengthening. Her orgasm struck and she clamped down on curve between his neck and shoulder. Her teeth broke skin at the same moment Javier bit her, a slight pinch of pain before pure ecstasy hit. A tidal wave of sensation and emotion that swept her into a blissful oblivion.

Chapter Fourteen

Just a week ago, had someone told Javier that having a woman mark him as mate would prove the most mind blowing experience of his life, he would have laughed. The moment it happened, though, he exploded, and not just with his cock. At the first taste of her coppery blood and the reciprocal pinch of her bite, something beautiful happened. He couldn't have said if it was the essence of his beast, his soul, or something else, but a part of him meshed with her, became inexplicably and intimately twined. In that moment, he knew her better than he knew himself, and the discovery of how much she'd had to fight to overcome her fear at joining with him did more than awe him, it made him love her with every atom of his existence.

In public, Naomi exuded a tough, no-nonsense persona; however, just as he'd suspected, Naomi was in actuality a softy at heart. He discovered while she perhaps claimed she feared a life of chaos if she mated with one of her kind, she feared even more not having the same kind of loving and close relationship her parents shared. Of just being a thing to her mate, not an equal and loved partner. A fear she'd never even admitted to herself and which she'd overcome enough to take the plunge and commit herself to not one, but two shifter males.

He could only clasp her tight as their bodies rode the wave of revelation where she too learned his inner secrets, such as the fact he already loved her for who she was, and would never do anything to hurt her. *This is forever, sweetheart.*

Their moment of complex unity faded as they returned to themselves and the shuddering of their spent bodies. His teeth released her skin at the same time as hers left his, and they laved the marked spot, slowing the sluggish flow of blood. Hugging her tight, Javier, usually such a smooth talker, couldn't think of any words grand enough to thank her for what she'd done, what she'd given him. All he could whisper, as he clasped her body to his, was, "I love you, sweetheart. Thank you for trusting me. I promise to be worthy of it."

She didn't reply, but her body trembled in his arms. It didn't bother him. He already knew everything he needed, and whether she admitted it aloud or not, he'd already seen in their moment of joining that she loved him, too.

It proved hard to let her go, but Javier understood he needed to. He formed only one part of the threesome. Ethan waited his turn, the trepidation on his face stemming from uncertainty and fear that perhaps she would leave him out. That she wouldn't want him. Javier knew better, and now Ethan deserved his turn at glory.

Javier rolled Naomi off his body onto her back. She opened eyes, still bright with wonder and gave him a soft smile. At his inclined head, she tilted her own and saw Ethan. Opening her arms wide, she beckoned him, and with a fierce expression of relief, Ethan covered her body, his lips claiming hers. Javier spent an indulgent moment watching them, admiring the passion that engendered no jealousy, but stirred his desire anew.

"Roll onto your back," Javier murmured, determined to aid his friend in reigniting Naomi's desire so he too might experience the ecstasy of the mating bond.

Complying, Ethan tilted, bringing Naomi with him, their lips never parting. Javier knelt beside them and ran a hand down her back, loving how her lush body complemented Ethan's thick one. He especially enjoyed the view of her rounded buttocks peeking up. Placing his hands on her rounded cheeks, he squeezed and kneaded them before sliding a hand between them and finding her cream soaked cleft.

A shudder went through her body when he rubbed his finger against her clit, then another as he slowly stroked it, her arousal stirring at his touch. "Get on your knees, sweetheart," Javier ordered.

Her lips still latched to Ethan's, she obeyed, letting her knees drop to either side of Ethan's hips and pushing her bottom up. Javier straddled his friend's legs and felt his own cock twitch at the pink and perfect view of his mate's—*my woman's*—cleft. He wasn't one of those men who could go down on a woman when she dripped with cum, but he had no problem stroking her. He thrust two fingers into her and almost moaned himself when her muscles clutched him tight. In and out, he pumped her, priming her need.

Below her eager pussy, Ethan's cock strained, thick and long, almost too thick which made preparing her for his shaft extremely important. Javier caressed her more intently, concentrating on her little nub until she squirmed and mewled, her body primed for penetration. Tugging on her hips, Javier lowered her onto his friend's cock, watching her pink sex engulf the wide shaft, slowly.

About halfway down Ethan's prick, she gasped. "Too big."

"No it's not," Javier soothed. "You'll soon see how hungry your pussy is for his big cock." Javier curved his arm around her hips and let his finger find her nub. With rapid strokes that had her crying out, he worked her until she was the one pushing herself down onto

Ethan's dick, swallowing his thick length until she sheathed him completely.

Poor Ethan, he fought to remain still as she adjusted herself to his size. His heavy body lay rigid on the bed, muscles bunching and taut with strain. Javier made things even harder by staying pressed against Naomi's backside, his finger not relenting on her clit, which surely caused her channel to spasm around Ethan's cock.

"Alright, sweetheart, time for you to come all over your big bear. Show him how sweet your pussy feels when it's climaxing."

They both moaned at his words, and Javier grinned. Watching them fuck was making him harder than a rock, but damn did he enjoy it.

Like Ethan had when their roles were reversed, he helped Naomi ride Ethan, grinding and rocking her against him until their bodies coiled at the building bliss.

"Now, Naomi," he whispered. "Make him yours."

Her face already buried in Ethan's neck, she just needed to bite, and the moment she did so Ethan let out an exultant bellow before returning the favor.

Javier watched as their bodies shuddered in the throes of climax, writhed as something magical struck them, an esoteric and life changing force that he could almost see sparkling in the air.

Draping himself over her prone body, he hugged the two people he would spend the rest of his life with. *And if I might say, I think Fate chose damned well.*

* * * * *

Ethan wanted to roar in glee. He wanted to beat his chest from the tallest building and shout to the world that Naomi was his mate. And even better, she loved him. She hadn't said it yet, of course, but in their moment of joining, he'd seen it. Seen how she trusted him. Seen how even despite his own misgivings about himself, she cared for him.

She'd chosen him.

It made him want to throw himself on his knees and worship her. On second thought, as her mate, he had every right to revere any part of her he desired.

How freakn' awesome.

Of course, first they needed to revive her. She lay on the bed between him and Javier, her eyes shut, her cheeks flushed and her chest still heaving.

"I guess baby here is going to need some time to recuperate," Ethan commented.

"Well, you know, she is an intellectual, not a jock like us," Javier added with a grin.

"Seems a shame to let the nice hot tub go to waste, though. Maybe we'll just let her sleep a bit while we go and relax."

She pried one eye open. "Can't a woman bask in the afterglow? I mean, you both only had one orgasm each. I, on the other hand, enjoyed a glorious two."

"She's right. That does seem unfair. Especially after she promised us some display of her oral skills," Javier teased.

"Ha, I think she's backing down from that promise now because she doesn't think she can handle my cock," Ethan boasted.

"I know what you're doing," she grumbled, her lips twitching into a smile. "And it's working. But first, let's clean them off in the tub. I am not into dirty dick."

Red heat stained his cheeks, which kind of matched Javier's shocked look, and their little vixen chuckled, obviously pleased at their reaction. She crawled off the bed over Ethan's body, sliding her skin over his which his sensitized body enjoyed way too much, especially his cock which twitched already in reply. His hands tried to clutch at her, but with a laugh, she evaded them and sashayed over to the hot tub. As she bent over to run a hand through the water, she afforded them a delectable view of her ass and the shadow between her thighs.

A sigh of pleasure escape him. "How did we ever get so lucky?"

"I have no idea, my friend. But let's not waste a moment."

Stepping up the single step, Naomi sank into the liquid and closed her eyes in pleasure. Ethan bounded out of bed on silent feet and made his way to her. A quick jab at a button and a rumble started up as the jets came on. The motion made her start and she opened her eyes, eyes already bright with erotic intent. A soft growl escaped him at the invitation she threw their way, one he and Javier accepted.

They closed in on her on either side, and with nowhere to go—and he could tell she didn't really have any desire to flee—she let them catch her. Their hands roamed her body, skimming the surface of her silky skin, never lingering in one spot too long. A gentle tease for his fragile flower. She closed her eyes as they stroked her, their slick and naked bodies brushing hers as they explored. Their cocks, already hard again, butted against her, one on each side as he and Javier teased her with their readiness.

Her slick hand grasped him, and through slitted eyes, he saw she'd also grabbed hold of Javier. She pumped them in the water and Ethan closed his eyes at the sensual pleasure of her touch.

She leant into him, raising her lips, and he bent his head for her. "I want to suck your cock," she told Ethan, nipping at his earlobe. "I want to see how much of that big dick of yours I can take in my mouth." That almost made him cum. Of course, what she wanted to do to his cock couldn't be done in the water—not unless she was a mermaid. But he wasn't about to say no to a display of her oral skills.

Grasping her slick body, he threw her over his shoulder, and in seconds they were back on the bed.

Heaven couldn't feel any better than Ethan did at that moment. First, he'd enjoyed mind blowing sex with Naomi. Then she'd marked him and he'd gotten to see just how much she loved him the way he was. And now she crawled up between his thighs, her gaze purposeful and her full lips beckoning. His cock twitched in response and she pounced on it, drawing a cry, unbidden from his lips as she engulfed his head in one wet swoop.

She sucked him like a lollipop, slurping and sucking at his sensitive cockhead. Every now and then she'd stop and swirl her tongue around his length, licking every inch of his shaft before popping him back into her mouth. Warmed up, she got bolder, drawing his thick prick into her mouth, bit by bit, stretching wide. She couldn't take him all the way, but he appreciated her effort. He twined his fingers in her hair as she worked him, hissing in pleasure as her teeth grazed his skin.

At her sudden mewling sounds around his cock, Ethan looked over her bobbing head to see Javier, bent over with his face buried between her cheeks, eating her sweet pussy. She groaned and growled as she continued to blow him, the vibrations of her pleasure cries making him tremble.

"Javier," he gasped. "You've got to have a turn. She's got the most amazing mouth."

His friend lifted his face from between her legs and knelt up, slapping his hard cock off her buttocks. "Mmm, you were so right about her tasting like honey. I've got her primed for some cock. Fuck her hard would you while she sucks me."

Naomi moaned in reply, releasing Ethan's cock with a wet popping sound. "You guys are so fucking dirty. Have I mentioned I love it?"

Javier slapped her ass before shifting positions with Ethan. He watched for moment, shafting his own dick, as her head descended on Javier's. His friend's eyes closed and his lips parted on a sigh as her head bobbed. Ethan felt his balls tighten in response at the erotic display. Moving to kneel behind her, he found himself captivated by the sight of her gleaming pink sex. Her could smell her arousal, see it, and he couldn't resist leaning in for a taste giving her one long, wet swipe of his tongue.

Positioning himself, with his cock poised at her slit, he first rubbed himself against her, wetting the tip of his cock with her juices. Around and around, he swirled his dick, inserting only the tip and then pulling back, wanting her good and ready for him.

"Dude," he heard Javier exclaim in a pained voice. "Would you fuck her before she bites my dick off?"

With a chuckle, Ethan thrust into her, not hard, but enough to sheath the first few inches. Her channel gobbled him up eagerly and tightened spasmodically around him. Ethan stilled, his fingers clutching at her ass cheeks, spreading them wide so he could watch as he slid the rest of his cock in.

Fuck did that feel good. The first time round, under the influence of the mating fever to mark her, he'd not truly had time to appreciate just how good it felt to be inside her. How right.

The second time around, though, fuck, he could possibly die from the pleasure of it. To distract himself as she brought Javier to the same brink he already rested on, he licked his finger and rubbed it against her tight rosette. Big mistake. Her whole body tightened, most especially her sex, which clamped down on his cock.

Ethan gasped, his hips jerking forward against her buttocks, ramming him deeper. She made a moaning sound and her head bobbed more frantically making Javier groan. An interesting chain reaction. Ethan poked at her tight ring again, prepared this time for her reaction, but it didn't make it any less pleasurable.

Carefully, he worked his finger into her anus, and her whole body bucked as her climax suddenly hit. Taken by surprise, Ethan began to pump his hips as his cock raced to catch her, milking her orgasm and triggering a second one. The spasming of her vaginal muscles just about drove him mad.

Through half lidded eyes, he saw Javier's hands, clutching at her head, pumping her up and down, her eager cries testament to her enjoyment of their actions. With a bellow and a final, deep seated thrust, Ethan came inside her, Javier's cry of release echoing only a moment later.

He collapsed on the bed, panting, Naomi's glistening body nestled to his side with Javier on the other.

And all she could manage to say was, "Wow." Then she giggled. They joined her in laughing, the moment so perfect and carefree he wished it would never end.

They made it last as long as they could. In between food, a shower and rounds three and four, they talked. Then fucked. Then talked some more which led to more lovemaking, until finally, their bodies sated and exhausted, they collapsed in a sweaty tangle of naked limbs. A perfect ending to a perfect day.

Chapter Fifteen

At brunch the following morning, Naomi, sore but happier—and more sated—than she'd ever imagined, ate her bacon while watching the people coming and going from the hotel restaurant. They hadn't left their room at all the previous day, much too occupied with *other* things. Really fun and sweaty things.

However, if they were to draw the thugs after her, she needed to make an appearance and make a bulls-eye of herself. Not as much fun as making love to her new mates, but even she had to admit her men needed some recovery time so they could play later that afternoon in the scheduled lacrosse match.

Ethan and Javier stood across the room talking to some team members, but they kept shooting her heated glances. She managed not to blush, but only barely as she remembered their promise before they'd come down.

"After we win the game, we're going to order up a bottle of champagne," Javier started.

"And pour it all over your naked, hot body," Ethan continued.

"We're going to lick it off your skin, and suck it off your sweet pussy."

"Then we're going to prep that tight little ass of yours and we're going to sit it on Javier's cock."

"As I teach you to enjoy some backdoor loving, Ethan's going to eat your soaking pussy, making you cum hard and as your body still trembles in climax and I fuck your tight ass—"

"I'm gonna slide my big cock into you and pump you until you scream and cum hard all over both our cocks. Then, we're gonna fuck you a little more, until you climax again."

Was it any wonder her panties were already soaked? She sighed as she realized just how totally screwed she was. Not only had they marked each other last night, but she liked the big lugs. More than liked actually, loved. Not that she'd said it aloud yet. The knowledge still kind of blew her away. Besides, she comforted herself with the fact they already knew after the whole marking thing.

Speaking of which, talk about rocking her world. Never before had she imagined knowing someone— make that two someones—so intimately. She'd learned Javier might have fucked all those women—*grrr*—but cared for none until he'd met her. It amazed her to realize in that moment of truth how he'd gone from being a roaming tomcat to a happily leashed one.

During her unity with Ethan, she discovered his doubts and insecurities about his size. Learned of his regret over his lack of suave manners and his joy over the fact that she didn't fear him. As if she could fear her big teddy bear.

Stirring her coffee, unsure of how many sugars she'd poured as she daydreamed, her wolf stirred in her mind and rumbled in warning as shrill feminine laughter split the air. Tilting her head up, she narrowed her eyes as she saw a cluster of young, nubile females clustering around her men. And the hussies dared to touch them. It didn't appease her to know they were human and couldn't scent that those two men in particular belonged to her.

A low growl spilt from her lips as one brazen slut—who was really asking to have her throat ripped out—rubbed her tits against Javier's arm while another pinched Ethan's butt. About to stand up, she watched in pleasure—and a little disappointment because she

182

wouldn't get to tear some hair—as her mates, extricated themselves from the females with shaken heads and walked away, toward Naomi.

Naomi smirked at the crestfallen females and then stood to give each of her men, a long, tongue-laced kiss.

Javier chuckled as he sat down. "Jealousy becomes you," he stated

"Was not."

"Liar," Ethan chided with a grin.

She stuck her tongue out. "Like you wouldn't be annoyed if some guy rubbed himself all over me?"

"I'd kill him, out of sight, of course, so as to not offend your delicate sensibilities," Ethan intoned as he snagged her last piece of bacon.

"Isn't that a little extreme?"

"Nope. It's different for men."

"And how is it different?" she asked crossing her arms and glaring at him.

"Double standard." He shrugged, while Javier snickered behind a hand. "You'll have to get used to it."

Shocked, it took Naomi a jaw-dropped moment before she realized the twinkle in Ethan's eye meant he teased her. She slapped his arm, which didn't do a thing to hurt him. Annoyed because both he and Javier were just about bent over double in mirth, she hit them where it hurt.

With a smirk meant to antagonize, she said, "Excuse me while I go back to our room to masturbate. Alone." They went scooting after her as she stalked away. The elevator held other patrons as they went up to their room, but that didn't stop her from leaning up to Ethan's ear and whispering, "I can't wait to get my hand in my panties. I am soooo wet."

183

At the sound of his strangled moan, she turned to Javier, but instead of speaking, she just winked and looked down at her cleavage wondering if he thought of what she'd done with her tits to him the previous night during round four.

When the elevator doors opened, she'd no sooner strutted off than Ethan scooped her up like a football and ran down the hall to the sound of her giggling. Javier sprinted past with the key card to let them in.

In the end, after a bit of groveling and laughter, she let them bring her off with their mouths and fingers, but no cock because, as she explained, as she lay between them naked and glowing afterward, "You need to save that pent up energy for the game."

"How am I supposed to play with this?" Javier moaned pointing to his rigid cock.

"Maybe you should think of joining a baseball team," she teased.

"Or maybe we should beat your sweet little ass with them instead?" Ethan growled, his eyes dancing with mischief.

"Ooh, that actually sounds like fun, but you still can't do it until after the game." At their resigned and identical sighs, she laughed, a mirth cut short as reality intruded. They'd discussed their plan to capture her assailants the night before, but caught up in the passion of discovering their bodies, she thought it prudent to go over it once more. "So tell me what I'm supposed to do again?"

"Just be yourself."

"Well, duh," she replied rolling her eyes. "Apart from that. How am I supposed to draw my attacker out?"

"We figure they'll try something at the game," said Javier.

"Um, but won't you guys be on the floor, not that I need any help," she added quickly.

"You won't be alone," Ethan replied cryptically.

"If you say so. What if they don't come after me like you think they will?" What she left unsaid was what if they went after her family or her mates instead?

"Call it a gut feeling," Javier answered, leaning over to kiss her temple.

"Don't worry," Ethan rumbled. "We won't let anyone hurt you."

"Ha, I'd like to see them try. Now, isn't it time you two lazy asses got ready for the match?" She bounced off the bed and stood with one hand on her cocked hip. "I've got a prize for the winners," she sassed as she traced a finger down her body to her cleft. She laughed at their matching groans.

As she dressed, a touch of trepidation—that she would never relay aloud—made her hope things would go as smoothly as her mates thought. But, if they didn't, then she'd do her damnedest to make sure they didn't get hurt.

*****

The boys seated her in the rapidly filling arena before leaving her to prep for the game. An excited buzz filled the air, and this time, with a vested interest in two of the players, she found it contagious.

Almost every seat in the place was taken, yet almost her entire row remained empty. As odd as it seemed, Naomi wondered if her men had arranged that as a buffer zone for her. *Or a lure to draw my stalker out?*

185

The two teams came out amidst wild cheering; Naomi joined in, along with some loud wolf whistles at the sight of number sixty-nine and forty-four. They must have heard her because Ethan's face split into a grin as he waved up at her, while Javier gave her a salute and a wink.

Everyone stood as the Canadian national anthem came on and the crowd sang. Shifters or not, they took great pride in their country, and she grinned as they sang "…glorious and free," so true when it came to shifters in this beautiful land.

Patriotism done, the teams assembled on the benches and the first line came out for a face off. With a shrill buzz, the game started. Naomi sat on the edge of her seat, eyes glued to the action.

At the beginning of the third period, the Loup Garou's led by two points and she wondered how she'd never noticed before what a truly fantastic sport lacrosse was.

My boys can crosscheck me, naked, anytime.

A bulky form sat next to her in the stands, interrupting her pleasant thoughts. She only sparred the stranger a quick glance, but it was enough for the late arriving patron to engage her in conversation.

"So you're the she-wolf leading the boys on a merry chase are you?"

Naomi, who had turned her attention back to the game, froze and turned back to regard the man. Boar, she corrected, her wolf scenting the man's beast; although, she could have probably figured that one out on her own given his close set eyes, brutish features and bulky body. "I'm sorry, but do I know you." Her heart sped up as she wondered if she finally faced the troublemaker behind all the mishaps.

" Maurice," he offered, thrusting out a thick hand. "I used to coach the boys when they were a part of my team in the prairies. Sadly, I didn't take them seriously when they told me they got an offer to come out east, and I've been trying to get them to come back ever since. I guess that won't be happening at all now since they told me they gone and found themselves a female."

"Yeah, well, you know there's no saying no to fate." The man, even though he seemed amiable enough, raised her hackles, both human and wolf.

"I've got to say, you're much braver than I would have cottoned given their reputation."

"Excuse me?"

"Surely you've heard? Those two are real ladies men. Gosh, I don't think Javier's ever slept with the same girl twice, and well, that Ethan, he might seem like a great, big, old teddy bear, but he sure has a temper on him."

Her smile turned cold. "Really. I didn't know. Well, they say the mating bond changes a male."

"So you're planning on marking them?" His beady eyes narrowed and clanging bells went off in her head.

"Actually, it's already done." She angled her neck left and right, displaying the skin and he stared with knitted brows at her mating marks which shone with a silvery sheen. It was the only wound shifters received that always left behind a scar. "Well, it's been real nice meeting you, but if you'll excuse me, the ladies room is calling." Naomi stood up and made her way out of the auditorium, her heart racing.

Could they have gotten it wrong all this time? Did the threat come about because of her relationship with Javier and Ethan and not one of her clients after all? A desperate coach who seeing his ex-star players were settling down with a local girl would stop at nothing to get them back?

Her wolf yipped at her stunning conclusion and she hurried down the hall making her way to the locker room. It didn't surprise her to hear steps following. It's what they'd planned for.

She whirled and saw Maurice lumbering after her, and just a few feet behind, four hulking men who cracked their knuckles with menace.

"You just don't know how to take a hint," Maurice huffed, his beady eyes flashing with ire as he came even with her.

"Oh, yeah, like the clues you left were so clear. Maybe next time you should try actually phrasing it in terms people could understand."

"I should have just had you killed when I first had the chance," he spat. "You have been nothing but a pain in my ass."

"A fat ass that should have stayed in better shape," she retorted kicking out and connecting with his knee. His leg crumpled and he bellowed as she bolted.

"Get the bitch," he yelled. "I need her if we're gonna get the boys to come back."

Pounding feet and a quick glance over her shoulder confirmed pursuit by the four thugs, and she'd bet her collection of butterflies they were the same ones who'd beaten up her brother and shot Javier.

Ten feet from the locker room door and the hall's dead end, she skidded to a halt and whirled to face approaching shifters.

"Now boys, you really should reconsider. I am after all a delicate freakn' flower, and I abhor violence." Naomi planted her hands on her hips and tilted her head.

Maurice panted as he struggled to catch up. Approaching her and thinking he had her trapped, he leered. "Delicate, my fat ass. But even you, honey, ain't no match for five of us."

Naomi grinned as the door behind her swung open.

"No, but we are," Ethan growled as he came to stand by her side, Javier flanking the other.

Then the whole Loup Garou team poured out into the hall at her rear, while behind Maurice and his bully boys stalked her furious brothers, father and her mother who wore the most vicious snarl of them all.

Naomi blew the dead men a kiss. "Bye. Nice knowing you."

Maurice's piggy eyes darted around then back to her in fear. "Listen, maybe I was wrong to try and scare you off from the boys. Can't we come to a deal?"

"No," Javier said flatly. "No one hurts Naomi or her family." He flicked eyes gone stone cold her way. "Sweetheart, you need to look away. This might get messy."

"Please, baby, go somewhere else. I don't want to upset you," Ethan growled through gritted teeth. Held inside by only a tendril of will, his beast made his body pulse and bulge with a need to act.

How sweet of them to consider her dislike of chaos, however sometimes, a little bit of violence just couldn't be avoided. "I'll only be upset if you let these bastards walk out of here. Get 'em boys."

Permission granted, Ethan tore into the bastards along with her family while Javier handled Maurice himself with hard and quick jabs that bloodied his face. The rest of the team formed a circle around the scuffle, joined by the Toronto team. Along with Naomi, they watched and cheered as the shifters dispensed their version of justice. It wasn't pretty, but it formed a part of who she was. Who they all were, and she found a sense of relief in not fighting her more violent side. Heck, this was one time she wholly embraced it.

When it was all over except for the groaning—by the bad guys, of course—she couldn't resist singing "Nah-nah-nah-nah, nah-nah-nah-nah, hey, hey, hey, goodbye," as they carted out their limp forms.

Bad guys disposed of and their adrenaline pumping, the two lacrosse teams went back out to finish the match. Naomi, flanked by her screaming brothers, hollered the loudest, especially when a large Toronto player rammed into Javier, knocking him flat.

"Kill him, Ethan," she freaked, standing on her seat and shaking her fist. "Pound his sorry ass into that floor or I swear I'll come down and rip him a new one myself." Her bear roared in acknowledgement and took off in a deadly charge at the player she had her sights on. The crash made the Toronto fans wince, but Naomi's face split with a feral grin.

Okay, I admit I'm starting to get the whole sports thing. Now if only they'd hurry up and win, because watching them grunt, sweat and hit things was really turning her on.

The Loup Garou's won by a margin of three goals. Naomi whooped and hollered, barely avoiding a fistfight with a Toronto groupie. She could have taken the skinny bitch, but her brother Stu tossed her over his shoulder and carted her out. She let him, in too good of a mood to hurt Stu who apparently just followed her mates' orders. Besides, she needed to keep her energy for later.

She had two hot jocks to congratulate. When they took too long to come out, she marched into the sweaty locker room to the groans of her brothers and the cat calls of the scantily dressed players.

"What is taking you so long?" she yelled when she didn't immediately see them.

"Naomi!" Ethan's bellow carried out of the shower room along with clouds of steam.

Smiling, she leaned against the locker that smelt just right and waited. Dripping wet and wearing only towels around their loins, her hot studs came stalking toward her with glowering expressions.

A coy grin tilted her lips as she let her eyes rove appreciatively over their bodies. "Mmm, is that for me?"

"I thought her brothers were supposed to keep her out of trouble," grumbled Ethan as he shrugged on a shirt which Naomi smoothed down, using it as an excuse to touch to him.

Naomi snorted. "Ha. I'd like to see them try. Now would you hurry up and dress so we can get back to the hotel and get naked."

That got them moving, and when Ethan, still pumped from the fight and game, tossed her up over his shoulder, smacking her bottom when she protested, she grinned against his back.

Oh, yeah ,totally loving this jock thing now.

Javier made a detour when they hit the hotel, leaving her alone with Ethan who'd finally put her on her feet so as to no startle the humans in the hotel. As they went up the elevator, she tilted her head up to kiss him, but the jerk stayed out of reach. When she would have climbed him, determined to get a taste, he held her

191

immobile, stretching her arms above her head as his smoky eyes stared down at her.

"Kiss me," she begged.

"I don't know. You were a bad wolf coming into the locker room like that."

"But I wanted to see you," she pouted, only for a second before her lips curled into a grin.

"Vixen."

"Bite me."

The elevator dinged and he loosened his grasp. Slipping free, she took off down the hall, laughing then screeching as he scooped her up with one arm.

"Show off," she giggled as he balanced her while opening the door.

"Admit it, you want me for my body," he teased as he tossed her onto the bed.

She lay propped on her elbows and pretended to eye him up and down. "Mmm, your body, your cock, but I most especially want your mind."

In a flash, his body covered hers, and he clutched her into an almost literal bear hug. "I love you, Naomi."

"Show me."

He'd just finished stripping her down when Javier showed up wagging a bottle of champagne at her. "I seem to recall a plan that involved drinking this from our new cup."

Gaping at him, Naomi shook her head and giggled. "You know, if you do that, you'll probably end up with a bill for a new mattress from the hotel."

Javier shrugged. "I don't know about you, dude, but I think pleasuring our mate like we promised is well worth that price."

"She's worth the world," Ethan growled.

Javier held the bottle over her and prepared to tip it. Naomi screeched. "Wait! If you soak the bed, where will we sleep? Can't we save the champagne for after?"

"After what?"

"Well, wasn't there mention of…" She actually blushed, unable to say the words aloud.

"Yes?" Javier smirked at her as she squirmed on the bed.

"You're going to make me say it, aren't you?"

"Yup."

She glared at them both. "Fine. I want to try that whole sandwich thingy."

"In that case, I think we can agree to hold off on pouring the champagne. Ethan?"

"I don't know. Depends on if I get her ass."

"What? No fucking way. Have you seen the size of your cock?" she screeched.

Her mates just about died of laughter. Disgusted with their joke, she drew her knees up, exposing her cleft, licked one finger and inserted it.

Their mirth dried up instantly. "You know," she said conversationally as she dipped her finger in and out. "You're both awfully overdressed for what I want you to do to my body." Shreds of clothing went flying. "Ooh, that was quick. And lucky me, you're both ready to go."

More than ready, bobbing and eager. She knelt up on the bed and held out her arms to Ethan who slid into them, clasping her nude body against his, his hands sliding from her waist to her ass cheeks, squeezing them. Javier slid in behind her and pressing his hard body against her backside. The tip of shaft poked at her buttocks and she couldn't help tensing.

Javier chuckled and his warm breath feathered her ear. "So jumpy. Don't worry, sweetheart. We won't hurt you, but we will make you scream."

A reply proved impossible as Ethan caught her lips with his and forced her lips apart so he could insert his tongue. She sucked on it, knowing how much he enjoyed it by the low growls she swallowed.

Not to be left out, Javier pushed aside her hair and nipped the sensitive spot on the back of her neck. Caught between their naked bodies, her nerve endings tingling and her cleft trembling with desire, she lost herself in the overload of delicious sensations.

Behind her, Javier fell away and she heard the sound of a drawer opening. Ethan, his mouth still latched to hers, gripped her ass cheeks and spread them. She wondered why until she felt a finger covered in some kind of lotion rubbing at her rosette.

Clenching against intrusion was a natural reaction for her, but it didn't seem to bother Javier, who worked his finger slowly into her tight ring. His second hand found her clit and he pinched it before rubbing it. Soon, he had her rocking her hips back against the finger penetrating her, his clitoral stimulation easing the way into her backdoor.

The finger in her ass was joined by a second, and she gasped at the tight stretching feel of it. As if sensing her uncertainty, Ethan's lips left hers and found her taut nipples. He engulfed one, sucking on the erect peak while the finger on her clit rotated faster.

In no time at all, she again found herself pushing back against the dual penetrating digits, the discomfort gone and excitement taking its place.

Ethan's hands slid up her buttocks to settle around her waist. Lifting her with effortless ease, he held her up over Javier's groin, just high enough for Javier's prick to butt up against her ass.

"Ready?" Ethan asked in a soft rumble.

She nodded her head and immediately felt the hard head of Javier's prick pushing at her ring. She tried not to clench but couldn't help it. As if sensing her dilemma, Javier's hands took the place of Ethan's, holding her up and controlling the slow, excruciatingly slow descent onto his prick.

In front of her, Ethan lay almost flat, his body between Javier's legs, and thus, her own. He licked his way up her thigh to her cleft, his heated gaze holding hers the entire time. He blew on her sex, torturing her, and at the same time relaxing her which allowed Javier to sink a little further. When Ethan's lips brushed her clit, her pussy lips trembled as her honey seeped from her. He lapped at her, a wet lick that sent a ripple through her sex, a precursor to the climax to come.

Spreading her lips, his tongue delved into her sex, and the molten pleasure of that touch relaxed her enough to allow Javier to fully seat himself with a grunt.

The sensation was odd, but the more Ethan tongued her, the more she forgot the strangeness and soon found herself squirming instead.

"Ethan," she heard Javier gasp. "If we're going to do this together, get inside, because I can't hold it much longer."

Now trepidation did clutch her, as Ethan moved to kneel between their legs. Javier's hands, pulled at her, easing her back, making her very aware of his cock in her ass, and she couldn't help but stared at Ethan's huge one approaching her sex.

"Don't worry, baby," Ethan murmured. "It's going to feel good."

195

Looking up into his soft brown eyes, she nodded. She knew she could trust him not to hurt her.

The head of his cock poked at her. Already wet and ready, it slid in, and then in further, and holy fuck, it was insane. Tight and so full, her body felt like it would burst, but with pleasure, not pain. Ethan pressed further into her, his heavy body braced above hers while she lay back against Javier's. Sandwiched and fucked, so gloriously fucked.

With a controlled pace, Ethan thrust into her, back and forth, a seesawing motion that made her moan. He placed his hands on her hips to guide the pace and somehow he managed it so when he thrust in, Javier's cock did as well, sheathing them both deep inside her. It was freakn' incredible. She couldn't have stopped herself from climaxing if she tried.

Rapture took over as her body succumbed to wave after pleasurable wave. And still, they kept fucking her, their dual pumps into her body rolling her mind-shattering orgasm into a second screaming one.

Drifting in a state of boneless bliss, she assumed they came. She couldn't be sure. She did know she wore a stupid smile on her face and would probably never walk again. But that was okay, she had every confidence that Ethan and Javier would take care of her. *Lucky me.*

And in the end, they did end up wetting the bed with champagne, but hot damn, it was worth every incredible moment.

Epilogue

Two months later…

Naomi kicked the stove as the flame on the gas burner sputtered then died. Again. Stupid thing would need replacing. Not exactly a surprise given the home they'd bought just down the street from her parents still resided in the seventies. But, they'd gotten it for a great deal, and slowly but surely her men were remodeling and modernizing it. The master bedroom and bath were the first to get retrofitted into a decadent haven with the largest bed she'd ever seen and a walk in shower that could accommodate a hell of a lot more than just washing. The kitchen was the next room waiting for a makeover, not that she cared. She tried to do as little food poisoning as possible.

A timer beeped and Naomi, her tummy in knots, peered at the result. *Oh shit.* Well that would make dinner interesting.

Following the sound of grunting as her mates took on her five brothers in a game of lacrosse out back, she left the kitchen to exit onto her back porch. She paused for a moment to watch her men's shirtless sweaty bodies as they twisted and ran, taunting her brothers as they passed the ball back and forth down the makeshift field. In a dirty move, Chris tripped Javier just as he lobbed the ball. Heads swiveled to watch the stray ball's path, and she had a moment to appreciate their "Ooh'" of horror before she held up a frying pan and deflected the shot.

Seconds later brawny arms swept her up, surrounding her in a familiar, musky scent. Ethan's soft brown eyes peered down into her. "Sorry about that, baby. You okay?"

She rolled her eyes at his misplaced concern. No matter how many times she showed Ethan the tough stuff she was made of, he still persisted in treating her like a delicate princess—and she loved it. "It didn't even touch me. But if you want to apologize, then feel free to do so later in our bedroom." She winked as she said it.

His answering grin made her tummy tingle in a way that seemed to increase rather than diminish since they'd joined as mates. Javier came jogging up, looking sheepish.

"Sweetheart, I swear it wasn't my fault. He made me do it." Javier pointed a finger at Chris who gestured back rudely.

Everyone laughed. "You can join Ethan in apologizing later on your knees, naked. But the reason I came out was because I thought you'd both want to be the first to know I'm pregnant."

She didn't couch it, or temper it any way. Just threw it out there and then smirked as she reaped the results.

"Get her a chair," Ethan bellowed.

"Do you need some water? Ice cream? Foot rub?" Javier asked.

"I'm pregnant, not on my death bed. But I am hungry, and the stove won't work." She held up the frying pan and laughed when she saw her brothers duck and take cover.

"We'll fire up the barbecue right away."

"Anything else, baby?" Ethan asked, nuzzling her cheek.

"Just one more thing, I've come to the conclusion, I love you both and—" She hadn't even finished when Ethan's lips swooped down over hers in a toe curling kiss.

It took him several moments before he let her up for air to say smugly, "I already knew that." He didn't even grunt when she stomped on his foot. "But it's nice to hear it. I love you, too, baby. So much," he whispered against her lips before Javier snatched her from him and whirled her around. He stopped a few swings in with a chagrined look.

"Shoot, I forgot about the baby. Are you gonna throw up?"

Naomi laughed. "No."

"Oh, good." Javier's lips planted over hers and made her breathless. "I love you, sweetheart. I think I have since the moment you tackled me in the garage and mauled me."

"Freak," she murmured with a smile.

He set her down on her feet and then both her mates planted wet kisses on her cheeks with a promised, "We're gonna make you say it again later," before they ran off whooping, "We're gonna be daddies and she loves us!"

Shaking her head at their boasting glee, she also grinned. She might not always manage to act like a lady, and she sometimes dished out as much violence as she condemned, but there sure was something to be said for being a delicate freakn' flower to a pair of big—sometimes nerdy—jocks.

Just wait until I tell them it's twins, she thought with a snicker.

The End

Author Biography

So you want to know a little about me? Well, I'm in my later thirties, married eleven years to a wonderful, supportive man—yes, he's a hunk—who gave me three beautiful, noisy children aged ten, seven, and five. I work as a webmistress and customer service rep from home, and in my spare time—of which there is tragically too little—I write, read, or Wii.

I was born in British Columbia, but being a military brat lived a little bit everywhere—Quebec, New Brunswick, Labrador, Virginia (USA), and finally Ontario. My family and I currently reside in the historic town of Bowmanville, about an hour or so out of Toronto.

Wow, was that ever boring! Now for the fun stuff.

I'm writing fantasy the way I like it—hot with a touch of fantasy. I enjoy writing stories that blur the boundaries between good and evil, and in some cases stomp all over that fine line. I tend to have a lot of sexual tension in my tales as I think all torrid love affairs start with a tingle in our tummies. My heroes are very male; you could even say borderline chest thumping at times, but they all have one thing in common. An everlasting love and devotion to the one they love.

Visit me on the Web for news on current and upcoming releases at http://www.EveLanglais.com

Thanks for reading, ☺ Eve

More Books by Eve Langlais

Published by Amira Press:
Alien Mate
Alien Mate 2
Alien Mate 3
Broomstick Breakdown
Dating Cupid
Defying Pack Law
His Teddy Bear
Scared of Spiders
The Hunter (Realm series)

Published by Liquid Silver Books:
Princess of Hell Series
Crazy
Date With Death
Hybrid Misfit
Last Minion Standing
Toxic
Wickedest Witch

Published by Cobblestone Press:
A Ghostly Ménage
Apocalypse Cowboy
Cleopatra's Men
Fire and Ice
My Secretary Series (BDSM shorts)

Published by Champagne Books:
Chance's Game (Realm series)
Take A Chance (Realm series)

Other titles:
The Geek Job
Accidental Abduction

Made in the USA
Lexington, KY
07 July 2012